Praise for
The Cranberry Cove Mysteries

"Peg Cochran has a truly entertaining writing style that is filled with humor, mystery, fun, and intrigue. You cannot ask for a lot more in a super cozy!"

—Open Book Society

"A fun whodunnit with quirky characters and a satisfying mystery. This new series is as sweet and sharp as the heroine's cranberry salsa."

—Sofie Kelly, *New York Times* bestselling author of the Magical Cats Mysteries

"Cozy fans and foodies rejoice—there's a place just for you and it's called Cranberry Cove."

—Ellery Adams, *New York Times* bestselling author of the Supper Club Mysteries

"I can't wait for Monica's next tasty adventure—and I'm not just saying that because I covet her cranberry relish recipe."

—Victoria Abbott, national bestselling author of the Book Collector Mysteries

Books by Peg Cochran

The Cranberry Cove Mysteries

Berried Secrets
Berry the Hatchet
Dead and Berried
Berried at Sea
Berried in the Past
Berried Motives
Berry the Evidence
Berried Grievances
A Berry Suspicious Death

The Lucille Mysteries

Confession Is Murder
Unholy Matrimony
Hit and Nun
A Room with a Pew
Cannoli to Die For

Farmer's Daughter Mysteries

No Farm, No Foul
Sowed to Death
Bought the Farm

The Gourmet De-Lite Mysteries

Allergic to Death
Steamed to Death
Iced to Death

More Books by Peg Cochran

Murder, She Reported Mysteries

Murder, She Reported
Murder, She Uncovered
Murder, She Encountered

Young Adult Books

Oh, Brother!
Truth or Dare

Writing as Meg London

Murder Unmentionable
Laced with Poison
A Fatal Slip

Open Book Mysteries

Murder in the Margins
A Fatal Footnote
Peril on the Page
A Deadly Dedication

A Berry Suspicious Death

A
CRANBERRY COVE
MYSTERY

Peg Cochran

A Berry Suspicious Death
Peg Cochran
Beyond the Page Books
are published by
Beyond the Page Publishing
www.beyondthepagepub.com

Cover design and illustration by Dar Albert, Wicked Smart Designs

ISBN: 978-1-960511-80-5

Chapter 1

"I now pronounce you man and wife." The minister smiled at the couple. "You may kiss the bride."

Jeff Albertson turned to Lauren and embraced her. He smiled, put his hand on her chin and tilted her head as his mouth came down on hers. The audience burst into applause. Several of the women, including Gina, Jeff's mother, pulled tissues from their purses. Monica Albertson also wiped a tear from her eye. Her half-brother was married. She still thought of him as her baby brother, and she'd always felt protective of him. That wasn't going to change because he'd acquired a wife, but now he would have Lauren looking after him as well.

The day was sparkling with clouds like puffs of cotton candy floating lazily in the sky. Jeff had wanted to be married at Sassamanash Farm. He had always said it was where his heart was and fortunately, Lauren had agreed. He had returned from a tour in Afghanistan bitter and with an injured arm. The cranberry farm had helped to put him back together again.

Today, two tents were set up alongside one of the cranberry bogs. It was September and the harvest was underway. The bog was as decked out as any of the wedding guests with red, pink and white cranberries bobbing on top of the water waiting to be harvested. They created a splash of color against the pale blue sky and the white tents flapping in the soft breeze.

Jeff and Lauren walked arm in arm down the aisle, the serious expressions that had befitted the solemnity of the ceremony now replaced with huge, ear-to-ear smiles. Lauren was wearing a simple lace and chiffon gown with lace sleeves and a bateau neckline. It swirled around her legs as she walked and her floor-length tulle veil billowed out behind her.

While Monica greeted guests in the reception line, several men in jeans and shirts with *Dare to Dream Event Rentals* printed on them were already hard at work removing the chairs from the smaller tent and installing a wooden floor for dancing after the meal had been served.

Jeff and Lauren were greeting an older woman in a pale blue dress when Monica's stepmother Gina approached her and grabbed her arm. Despite having known Gina for years, her outfit still surprised Monica and she had to blink twice at it—an emerald green metallic jumpsuit with a low V-neckline and palazzo pants. It made Monica feel almost dowdy in her plum-colored wrap dress, which had seemed so elegant when she'd found it on sale at Danielle's Boutique in town.

Gina's eye makeup was slightly smeared as if she'd been crying and she held a crumpled tissue in her right hand.

"I see the ceremony made you tearful, too," Monica said, brandishing her own handkerchief.

Gina sniffed and pressed the tissue to her nose. "It was so beautiful but I can't believe my baby boy is married. It makes me feel so old."

"Don't be silly. You don't look a day over . . ." Monica hesitated. *How old was Gina anyway?* She finally settled on thirty-five and that seemed to make Gina happy. She let out her breath in relief.

A slight man with a shaved head, one gold stud earring, a set of brightly colored beads around his neck and a jacket with a Nehru collar hovered nearby. Gina put her hand on his arm and pulled him over.

"I want you to meet Kiran," she said. She turned her head and smiled at him. "He's responsible for this." She made a sweeping motion encompassing her body.

Monica tried not to stare. What on earth was Gina talking about? And who was Kiran? Was that his real name? Did he have a last name?

Gina kept her hand on Kiran's arm. "He owns the Soul Spring Spa that moved into that empty storefront on Beach Hollow Road next to the Golden Scoops."

Kiran's mouth quirked into a half smile. "Bit of irony, isn't it? A weight-loss spa next to an ice cream parlor."

His voice was soft—barely above a whisper—and with a hint of a lisp.

"He runs the most amazing weight-loss program." She glanced at Monica again. "You must try it."

What was she insinuating? Monica looked down at herself. She thought she looked quite good considering she'd given birth only a few months ago. The saleswoman in Danielle's had assured her that the dress she bought was flattering to her figure.

"He's the only practitioner in Cranberry Cove and the only one in the entire state of Michigan who has a Thermo, a brand-new technique that uses lasers to shape and contour the body along with his unique exercise classes." Gina ran a hand over her hips. "And he has a line of supplements called Thermodynamics that help rid the body of fat." She gave a self-satisfied smile. "I'm going to become one of his Soul Spring Ambassadors."

Monica tilted her head. "Meaning?"

"I'm going to be selling Thermodynamics. Kiran says I can make a fortune. All I have to do is recruit other ambassadors to work under me. Sort of like that company that sells candles." She snapped her fingers. "I can't think of the name but you know what I mean."

She certainly did. Her mother had been ensnared by them and had lost money rather than made it. It seemed not everyone wanted to buy or sell candles with seasonal scents named Fallen Leaves and Peppermint Patty.

Waitstaff began to circulate with round trays of sparkling wine and platters of hors d'oeuvres. Gina's husband, the owner of the Pepper Pot Restaurant in town, had offered to cater the event at a very reasonable price and Mick, the newest baker on Monica's staff, had been more than thrilled to provide the wedding cake.

The cake was a masterpiece—three tiers covered in swirls of buttercream garnished with sugared cranberries and red roses nestled on top.

A plump and pretty waitress with blond hair piled on top of her head and a name tag that read *Heather* offered them a tray of bite-sized quiches. Monica took one, but Gina shook her head, holding her glass of sparkling wine to her chest as if she was afraid it was going to be snatched away before she was finished.

"Excuse me," Monica said, giving Gina's hand a squeeze.

She'd spotted Nora in the crowd clustered under the tent. Nora ran the farm store and Monica never stopped being grateful for her. She was wearing an A-line dress with short sleeves in a very becoming lavender. Monica was so used to seeing her in corduroy pants or khakis and one of her collection of sweatshirts with sayings on them like *Motherhood Isn't for Sissies* that she almost didn't recognize her.

Monica made her way through the crowd toward her. "Nora! So glad you could come."

"I wouldn't have missed it for anything. It was all so lovely, wasn't it? Jeff looked so handsome and Lauren was positively radiant."

People were beginning to make their way to the round tables arranged under the tent. They were covered in white tablecloths printed with cranberries with rustic centerpieces of wheat grass, burgundy-colored spider mums and stalks of greenery. A long buffet table had been set up on one side for the wedding breakfast. A row of gleaming chafing dishes held the main course choices of cranberry-glazed chicken, mini beef Wellingtons and saffron risotto along with various vegetables and salads.

"I wonder why they call it a wedding breakfast?" a woman in a rust-colored silk dress said as she swept past Monica. She vaguely heard the woman's companion's answer. "It's the first meal the bride and groom will eat as a couple. It began in . . ." The remainder of his explanation trailed away.

Monica spotted Gerda and Hennie Van Velsen, the identical twin sisters, headed her way. They both looked charming in matching calf-length dresses in a burgundy tapestry print.

Hennie squeezed Monica's arm. "It's all so lovely, dear."

Gerda patted her fluffy white curls. They'd both obviously had their hair done for the occasion.

Indeed, it looked as if all of Cranberry Cove had donned their best for Jeff and Lauren's wedding. Tempest Storm, the owner of Twilight, was wearing a caftan in a deep blue brocade shot with silver threads. She was sipping a glass of sparkling wine and chatting with Bart Dykema, who ran the butcher shop in town. Monica almost didn't recognize him without the apron he always had tied around his waist.

Greg was beginning to shepherd people to the buffet line, where waitstaff stood poised to serve the contents of the various chaffing dishes and platters.

Monica finally joined them and made her way to the table where Gina, Kiran and her mother, Nancy, were already seated. Monica thought her mother looked lovely in a garnet scroll print sheath with a matching jacket. She looked from Nancy to Gina and back again. The two women couldn't have been more different and yet her father had married both of them, one after the other. She shook her head. It was something she'd probably never understand.

As soon as everyone had quieted down, Jeff's best man, Brian Davis, who had been in the Army with him, gave a heartfelt toast, leaving Jeff reaching for a handkerchief to wipe his eyes. Other speeches followed and the guests began to eat.

The rest of the meal seemed to go by in a blur and Monica could only imagine how Jeff and Lauren felt. They were both already standing by the table that held the wedding cake and Jeff had been handed a huge knife with a crystal handle. With Lauren's hand over his, he sliced through the first tier of the cake. A round of applause burst out.

Monica noticed Mick and a woman she didn't recognize moving toward her.

"The cake is a masterpiece, Mick. You've outdone yourself."

Mick beamed with pride.

The woman with him edged closer and Mick took her by the arm.

"I'd like to introduce you to my wife, Jolie Spencer. He looked slightly sheepish. "I guess she's Jolie Amentas now."

Monica was so startled she didn't catch the woman's first name. "I'm sorry, your name is . . . ?"

"Jolie. It means pretty in French." She patted her hair.

When Monica hired Mick to help out in the farm kitchen, he hadn't been married. And that had only been a couple of months ago. A lot of women in Cranberry Cove were going to be disappointed. Mick's Greek god good looks had all the females in town drooling over him.

Jolie appeared to be well into middle age with a voluptuous figure nearly spilling out of her dress and a beehive's nest of teased blond hair. She had diamond studs the size of dimes in her ears, which had obviously been given to her by someone else or were well-made fakes. Certainly, Mick couldn't afford jewelry like that on his salary.

"Congratulations," Monica managed to mumble.

Silverware tapping against glasses created a melodic tinkling sound that filled the tent.

"Look." Mick pointed toward the cake. "Jeff and Lauren are about to feed each other."

There was no stuffing cake in each other's face and Monica was relieved. Not that she had expected either Jeff or Lauren to do something like that.

"I'd better go plate the rest of the cake," Mick said, scurrying off. Jolie drifted away as well, leaving behind the mingling scents of vanilla and jasmine.

"Would you care to dance?" Monica's husband, Greg Harper, appeared in back of her and whispered in her ear.

She turned, looked up at him and smiled. He was terribly handsome in his new suit and tie, so unlike the casual khakis and sweaters he wore every day to his shop Book 'Em. His dark hair was slightly rumpled, and she reached up and pushed back a lock that had fallen onto his forehead. "I'd love to dance."

As Greg led her onto the dance floor, his hand on the small of her back, she noticed Gina dancing with Kiran. The DJ had switched to an upbeat pop song and Gina was really letting loose. Monica hoped she wasn't going to hurt herself.

The song ended and Kiran began to walk away. He bumped into Jolie, leaving them both looking comically startled. Kiran nodded an apology and scurried off while Jolie swiped at her dress where some of her drink had splashed.

After smoothing her dress, Jolie made a beeline for Monica, her brow wrinkled and her mouth set in a thin line.

"I need to talk to you," she said.

"I'm going to get some water." Greg began to walk away and Monica turned her attention to Jolie. "Yes? What is it?"

"I think you should know," Jolie began, but before she could finish her sentence, she noticed Mick gesturing at her. She glanced at him and then back to Monica.

"I'm sorry. I think Mick needs me. I'll talk to you later," she whispered as she walked away.

• • •

In what felt like the blink of an eye, the wedding was over. A few people lingered, chatting, in small clusters on the lawn and one or two were still in their seats, but the waitstaff was already clearing off the buffet table, plunking dirty dishes and silverware into bus tubs with a clatter and bundling up tablecloths and napkins.

Gina was collapsed in her seat, her high heels kicked off to the side and her feet up on an empty chair.

Jolie was sitting with a young girl with blond hair and seemed to be having a heated discussion. Jolie got up suddenly and headed toward a row of boxwood topiary trees in decorative ceramic planters that had been brought in to obscure several white porta-potties. A young man from Johnny-on-the-Spot was meant to be collecting them momentarily.

Monica was rubbing her feet—she so rarely ever wore heels—when she saw Wilma coming toward her pushing Teddy in his carriage. She normally worked as Greg's assistant at Book 'Em, where she'd appointed herself general dogsbody and had been more than willing to step in as a babysitter.

"Someone's happy to see you," she said, smiling down at the baby, who was making faint cooing sounds and kicking his feet.

Monica's heart melted at the sight of him. It still felt like a miracle even after more than two months. His wispy hair was dark like hers and Greg's but he had Greg's blue eyes and long lashes. When she was pregnant, people had constantly asked, are you hoping for a boy or a girl? She honestly hadn't cared one way or the other, but now that Teddy was here, she couldn't imagine a more perfect baby.

She reached into the carriage, took him out and cradled him in her arms.

"Gitchy goo," someone said, and Monica looked up to see Janice leaning over the baby.

Janice also worked in the bakery with Monica and had been there slightly longer than Mick.

"It was a beautiful wedding," Janice said. She frowned. "Too bad they didn't have it on a Wednesday."

"Why on earth should they have?" Monica knew Janice believed a lot of superstitions, but this?

"You know what they say. Monday for wealth, Tuesday for health, Wednesday the best day of all, Thursday for losses, Friday for crosses, and Saturday no luck at all."

"That's ridiculous. Everyone gets married on a Saturday. It's an old wives' tale." Monica barely restrained herself from rolling her eyes. She didn't want to hurt Janice's feelings. What if she quit? The thought caused her heart to thump in panic.

Janice shrugged. "Suit yourself," she said in ominous tones.

Monica looked around. Nearly everyone had departed by now and the waitstaff was almost finished cleaning up.

A truck rumbled down the dirt road—not much more than a path worn in the earth—that had *Johnny-on-the-Spot* written on the side in large black letters with the picture of a porta-potty, its door open as if in welcome, underneath.

It came to a halt, the door opened, and a young man jumped out. He was blond and as thin as the sticks Monica threw for her dog Hercule. He had a cigarette dangling from the corner of his mouth.

He trundled a handcart over the uneven ground and disappeared behind the row of topiary trees.

Teddy began to fuss so Monica slipped her shoes back on and started to walk around, gently rocking him in her arms.

Out of curiosity, she wandered over to where the porta-potties were located and watched as the young man, who had *Timmy Fisher* embroidered on his blue work shirt, began to position the cart next to the first porta-potty. He stopped for a moment and swiped a hand across his brow.

The sun was no longer at its peak but the air was still warm with a slight touch of humidity.

The young man was tilting the porta-potty slightly to ease it onto the cart when the door swung open and a body fell out.

Monica's first thought was that someone had been using the porta-potty and hadn't secured the door properly, but then she realized that wasn't the case.

The body lay sprawled on the grass and Monica recognized it immediately.

It was Jolie Spencer, now Amentas, and she was clearly dead.

Chapter 2

Monica stifled her scream but the baby must have sensed her distress nonetheless and began to cry. "Shhh," she said, swaying back and forth in an attempt to comfort him. "Shhh, it's okay."

Timmy, the young man in the process of picking up the porta-potties, yelped and stumbled backward. "I didn't do nothing, man," he said. "I was just doing my job. She just, like, fell out."

"It's okay. No one is blaming you," Monica said soothingly.

Teddy's wails trailed off and briefly turned into hiccoughs. Monica heard footsteps and turned around to see Greg running toward her.

"I was taking down the balloons in those trees over there when I heard something. I thought maybe Teddy . . ."

His face was pale and Monica noticed his hands trembling. "But now I see it's . . ."

"Jolie. Mick's new wife." Monica half turned toward the tents. "We need to get Mick and we need to call the police."

"Do you think it's okay if I take the porta-potty away?" Timmy said. Some color had come back into his face. "The boss is going to have a fit if I'm late with it. There's another wedding tomorrow and they've ordered five of these."

Monica shook her head. "I'm afraid not. The police will want to examine it."

"But what do I tell my boss?" Timmy's voice had become a high-pitched whine.

"I'm sure he'll understand under the circumstances." Greg patted Timmy on the shoulder. "You look like you could use a glass of water."

"Nah. I'm okay. It was a shock, that's all. The only other dead body I've ever seen was my grandmother at her viewing. And they had her all fixed up and stuff."

Monica could tell he was already formulating a juicy story to tell his fellow workers at Johnny-on-the-Spot.

"What's happened?" a woman coming up behind Monica said breathlessly. She was the blond server named Heather. "That's my former stepmother," she said, pointing at the body. She began to shake.

"I'm so sorry," Monica said.

"Maybe you should sit down. I'll get you a chair." Greg turned, about to head toward the tent.

"I'm okay," Heather said. "It was a shock."

Greg pulled his cell phone from his pocket and dialed 911.

"Jolie was married to your father?" Monica looked down at Teddy. He had fallen asleep despite all the commotion.

Heather's mouth tightened. "Yes. She used to be Jolie Spencer until she married that . . . that Greek kid."

Mick was hardly a kid, Monica thought, but it was clear there were at least two decades' difference in his and Jolie's ages.

"Speaking of Mick, someone needs to get him."

"I'll get him." Greg put his cell phone back in his pocket. "The police are on their way."

Monica heard someone stifle a gasp and turned to see Wilma, her knuckles tightening on the handle of the baby carriage.

"What happened?" she whispered.

"Someone was taken ill. Perhaps you can bring Teddy back to the house and put him down in his bassinet?"

"Of course," Wilma said, without taking her eyes off Jolie's body.

Monica handed her the baby and she nestled him in the carriage, pulling a light blanket over him now that the air was turning cooler.

Monica watched as she wheeled the carriage over the grass toward the tents. Wilma had disappeared from view when Monica saw Mick come running toward them.

"What is it? What's happened. Greg said it was something about Jolie . . ." He looked down. "Is she ill? Should we call a doctor?"

Monica touched his hand. "I'm afraid it's too late for that. We've called the police."

"Why the police?" Mick looked alarmed. "She must have had a heart attack."

"It's standard procedure in cases like this." Monica heard a car's engine and swiveled around.

The brakes squealed; then the sound abruptly cut off. Moments later two patrolmen appeared running toward the porta-potty. One of them had a rather large belly that hung over his belt and jiggled with every step. Monica thought she'd seen him before directing traffic in downtown Cranberry Cove.

The other patrolman had a crop of acne on his chin and looked to be barely out of his teens. He quailed slightly when he saw Jolie's body sprawled on the grass.

He pushed his hat back on his head and rocked on his heels. He turned to his partner.

"What do we do now?"

He pointed to the yellow crime scene tape in the young man's hand. "We string some of that up and wait for the boss to arrive."

The kid rubbed the back of his neck. "But what if she had a heart attack or something like that?"

"We won't know that till the medical examiner gets here, and if the scene gets trampled, Stevens will have a fit." He motioned for the young man to begin unspooling the tape.

They were finishing when Stevens arrived. She looked pleased to see they had the scene blocked off.

If it was even going to be a crime scene. Mick might be right. Jolie could have had a heart attack, Monica thought, and all this might be for naught. But the medical examiner would know for sure.

"Do we know who she is?" Stevens said, bending down to look at the body.

"Jolie Spencer . . . I mean it's Jolie Amentas now," Mick said.

Stevens's head shot up. "Amentas? As in Gus Amentas?"

"I'm his nephew."

"He works with me here in the farm kitchen," Monica said.

"Can you tell me what happened?"

Monica explained how Jolie's body had fallen out of the porta-potty when Timmy tried to lift it onto his handcart.

Stevens looked around. "The young man is still here, I hope?"

"He's over there."

Monica pointed to where Timmy was sitting on the grass, his knees drawn up to his chest and his arms wrapped around them.

"I'll get to him in a minute." Stevens sighed. "There aren't any apparent marks on the body," she muttered as she circled the scene. "But I've called the ME and she'll be able to hopefully tell us more." She glanced at her watch. "She should be here any minute."

Stevens was wearing tan poplin pants and a white short-sleeved blouse. She rubbed her arms where Monica noticed goose bumps were sprouting.

"Had she been ill recently or did she have any medical conditions?" Stevens looked at Mick.

"I don't know. I don't think so." He fiddled with the gold band on his left hand.

"Ah, here she comes." Stevens stepped forward to greet the medical examiner, who had finally arrived.

She was an older woman with short gray hair, lines around her eyes and a brisk, no-nonsense manner. After a brief conversation with Stevens, she pulled a pair of gloves from her bag and put them on.

Monica looked away as she knelt and began to examine the body. There was no dignity in death. Several minutes later, they heard her knees crack as she stood up.

"No signs of trauma," she said, snapping off her gloves. "But I'll know more after I've done the autopsy."

"I'm going to interview the fellow from Johnny-on-the-Spot, although I doubt he'll know much of anything." Stevens sighed. "The rest of you can go sit down. I'll call you when I need you."

• • •

One by one, Stevens interviewed the remaining people at the wedding, including some of the caterers and the guests who still hadn't left, like Gina and Kiran. Some of them grumbled about the inconvenience and some of the others were clearly going to be dining out on the story for months to come.

Timmy squawked a bit about not being allowed to take the porta-potty back to Johnny-on-the-Spot but finally drove off after Stevens had told him he could go.

The caterers were loading the last of their things into their van and Heather was driving off in her Lexus, the wheels of her car churning up dust as she sped away. Monica hoped that meant that Stevens was nearly done with them. She was tired and cold, and the shock of finding Jolie's body was beginning to set in.

Finally, they were all allowed to go. Monica took Greg's hand and they walked back to the house.

Monica groaned as she kicked off her heels the minute she walked in. She waved to Wilma, who was sitting on the living room sofa scrolling through the messages on her phone, then tiptoed up the stairs to the nursery.

Teddy was sound asleep, his tiny hands curled into fists and his eyes moving back and forth under his closed lids. Monica wondered what he could possibly be dreaming about.

She stood and watched him for several minutes, then left the room and tiptoed back down the stairs.

"Teddy's sound asleep," she said.

Wilma smiled. "He went right down and hasn't made a peep since." She gestured toward the baby monitor on the coffee table. "I've been listening."

Monica sank onto the sofa as Greg paid Wilma and walked her to the door. "I don't know what we'd do without you," he said as she looked up at him with adoring eyes.

Monica stifled a giggle. It had been obvious from day one that Wilma had a crush on Greg.

Greg sighed and rolled his eyes as he closed the door behind Wilma.

"I know she can be a nuisance." Monica followed Greg into the kitchen. "But she's really been a big help."

"She is. And I really do appreciate it."

"I'm glad Jeff and Lauren were already off to Mackinac Island for their honeymoon when Jolie was found," Monica said to Greg as he put on some coffee. "It would have been a shame if they hadn't been allowed to leave. Jeff's crew all chipped in to give them a couple of nights at the Grand Hotel as a present."

"With any luck, we'll find out that Jolie had a heart attack or some other sudden medical problem that caused her death," Greg said as he carried their coffees into the living room. "And all the drama will be over."

"I hope so." Monica put her feet up on the coffee table. "Anything but murder would be a relief."

• • •

Monica was glad Jeff's wedding had been in the afternoon and she'd gotten to bed at a reasonable hour because Teddy's cries woke her before sunrise the next morning. He'd only woken her up once during the night for a feeding and she felt quite rested.

She changed him and was sitting in the kitchen feeding him when Greg walked in, yawning and rubbing his eyes. His hair was tousled and his face creased from sleep. Monica felt her heart give that little leap it always did when she realized how lucky she was that they had met.

"Teddy and I are going to get some fresh air and walk down to the farm kitchen."

Monica was technically on maternity leave but she still insisted on checking on things from time to time. Mick and Janice were perfectly capable of running the farm kitchen and Nora the farm store, but she liked to keep her hand in nonetheless.

It was a sparkling September day and she enjoyed the walk down to the farm store to say hello to Nora. Teddy had been sleepy after his feeding and hadn't offered any resistance when she'd put on the sweater Gerda Van Velsen had knitted for him in a soft blue yarn.

It was a clear day, still with a chill in the air but the sun was already promising to warm things up by midday. Monica passed the bog near where the wedding had been held. Everything had been cleared away and it was hard to imagine that two tents, tables and chairs and dozens of people had been there the day before.

The artificial topiary trees that had shielded the porta-potties from view had gone back to Dare to Dream Event Rentals, and Monica was able to see the porta-potty itself surrounded by crime scene tape flapping in the breeze.

Teddy had begun to doze off and was sound asleep in his carriage by the time Monica reached the farm store.

She was pleased to see that a couple of cars were in the parking lot and two women were leaving the store clutching bakery bags and cups of coffee. They were only open half a day on Sundays, when people often stopped in after church for some baked goods.

Nora must have seen her coming because she opened the door with a smile and Monica wheeled the carriage inside.

Two of the three small round tables they'd added to the store were occupied with people sipping coffee and eating the cranberry goodies Monica and her team baked fresh every day.

She wheeled the carriage over to the empty table and sat down.

She glanced around the store with a sense of pride. It had been barely functioning when she'd arrived in Cranberry Cove to help Jeff and now they had a gleaming professional kitchen with the equipment needed to produce enough baked goods for the store each day as well as their customers in town, like the Cranberry Cove Inn and the Pepper Pot. They were even doing business with a small chain of gourmet grocery stores. She'd run her own café in Chicago until a chain gourmet coffee shop had opened down the street and siphoned off most of her business.

Nora had arranged a charming display of the cranberry-themed items they'd decided to carry—tablecloths, napkins, place mats and aprons in fabrics festooned with cranberries. Monica had recently been looking into adding mugs and serving pieces to their inventory.

If things went well, they might even have to enlarge the store. She laughed. She was getting ahead of herself.

"What's so funny?"

Monica felt her face flush. "Oh, nothing really. Just daydreaming."

No one was waiting to be served so Nora perched on the seat opposite her, occasionally leaning over the carriage and exclaiming how adorable Teddy was.

"Would you like a cup of decaf?" she said. "I've put on a fresh pot."

"That would be lovely. And maybe a cranberry scone to go with it."

"Coming right up."

Monica was trying to stick to a healthy diet for Teddy's sake but the doctor had told her this wasn't the time to diet—you needed as much as an extra five hundred calories a day to nurse a baby. A cranberry scone sounded like the perfect way to add those calories.

Nora placed a steaming cup of coffee in front of Monica along with a scone, the top of which sparkled with sugar. She was about to sit down when a customer came in and she quickly slid behind the counter.

The customer picked up her order and turned to scan the room for a seat.

"Detective Stevens, Tammy," Monica called, waving a hand and motioning to the empty chair at her table.

Stevens carried her cup and plate over and sat down with a groan. A smattering of gray roots was showing in her hair and her face was slack with fatigue. She leaned over the carriage and smiled.

"He looks so peaceful. Mine was up half the night. Nightmares. Apparently, the babysitter let him watch a horror movie and he woke up dreaming of monsters." She peeked in the carriage again. "He looks like you," she said, adjusting his blanket.

Monica laughed. "It's split down the middle. Half the people think he looks like me, the other half thinks he looks like Greg."

Stevens shrugged. "His face will change as he grows. There's no telling who he'll end up looking like." She flicked a packet of sugar with her finger, tore it open and poured it into her coffee. She stirred it and took a sip. "Shame about yesterday. A death at a wedding of all things."

"Fortunately, the reception was winding down." Monica stirred her coffee absentmindedly. "Poor Mick. He must be devastated."

Stevens's napkin had slipped off her lap and she bent down to pick it up. "Had they been married long?"

"No. It came as quite a shock to me. Mick only began working for me a couple of months ago, and at the time, he'd just arrived in this country."

"On some sort of visa, I suppose."

Stevens broke off a corner of her cranberry bread. She raised an eyebrow. "He didn't seem to be too broken up about his new wife's death. Still. You can never tell. People handle their grief in different ways."

"Have they performed the autopsy yet?"

Stevens hesitated. She took a bite of her cranberry bread and chewed. Finally, she said, "It will be all over the newspapers tomorrow so there's probably no harm in telling you. The medical examiner found that Mrs. Amentas had been suffocated. Traces of cloth fibers were found on her face and in her mouth. The killer must have smothered her, then shoved her into the porta-potty hoping she wouldn't be found for hours, which would make it harder for us to solve the case."

"That's dreadful." Monica put her coffee cup down so forcefully, it clanked against the table. "Had she been dead long when the young man from Johnny-on-the-Spot came to collect the porta-potties?"

"The ME can't pinpoint the exact time but believes she hadn't been dead for much more than an hour."

Teddy whimpered and moved restlessly in his carriage. Monica glanced at him but he had settled back down and was still sleeping.

"I know I've already interviewed you, but has anything come

back to you that might be significant? Do you remember seeing Jolie before she was killed?"

The wedding and reception ran through Monica's mind like a film strip. When had she last seen Jolie?

She thought it was before Wilma brought Teddy out to her. She was seated at the table and . . . Yes! She remembered seeing Jolie get up and walk toward the porta-potties. What had she been doing before? Monica scrunched up her eyes in an effort to bring the scene in her mind into focus.

"Yes!" She quickly glanced at Teddy but she hadn't woken him. "Jolie was seated at her table and she was talking to someone. A woman with blond hair."

"Young or old?" Stevens pushed her empty plate away.

"I couldn't tell exactly. Certainly not old. Not particularly young either. Maybe around thirty or so?"

"You don't know who she was?"

Monica shook her head. "I'm afraid not. I've never seen her before. Maybe she was a friend of Jeff or Lauren's."

"Jolie and this woman were talking?"

"Yes. But the discussion seemed . . . heated, or somewhat unpleasant. They appeared to be arguing about something." Monica remembered how the woman's chandelier earrings had whipped back and forth as she shook her head.

"And then what happened?"

"Jolie got up and began to walk toward the porta-potties. Or at least it looked as if that was where she was headed."

"What about the blond she'd been talking to?"

Monica tried to remember but it was futile.

"That was when Wilma wheeled Teddy down in his carriage and I'm afraid all my attention was on him."

"That's okay." Stevens pushed her chair back. "That's quite helpful. Hopefully, we can identify that woman by process of elimination."

"Who would do something so horrible? Suffocate someone and then leave them to die?" Monica thought she'd never get used to murder no matter how many times she was exposed to it.

"Don't worry. That's my job and I intend to find out."

Chapter 3

Monica passed the farm kitchen on her way back to the house. She was surprised to see a light was on. Had Janice forgotten to turn it off or was she still there? She decided to check. They only baked enough on Sundays to keep the farm store supplied until midday when it closed. Their biggest rush was in the morning after church services ended and trickled off the later it got.

Mick was obviously going to be on leave for a bit. He needed time to process the death of his wife, especially since it occurred in such a gruesome manner. Murder. She could never understand what drove people to it.

Mick and Jolie had seemed like such an unlikely pair, and not only because of the age difference between them. Besides, how long had they known each other before they got married? Why such a hasty decision? Jolie had seemed awestruck by Mick's good looks but Mick could have had his pick of almost any single woman in town.

Monica tried the door handle, and it turned. She wheeled the carriage over the threshold and shut the door. The kitchen was empty but she heard a voice coming from the storage area. That was strange. It sounded like Mick. What was he doing here?

Teddy was asleep so she maneuvered his carriage next to the counter and put on the brake. She glanced down and noticed a business card sitting out on top. She picked it up.

It was from La Nourriture, a well-known restaurant in Chicago whose chef had been lured away from a Michelin starred restaurant in Paris. What was Mick doing with it? Had he been planning to take Jolie there? On a honeymoon perhaps?

Mick was obviously on the telephone. Monica didn't want to eavesdrop but she couldn't help overhearing his conversation. She debated leaving when something caught her attention.

"Will I still be getting my green card now that my wife is dead? La Nourriture won't hire me without it and I'll be deported otherwise."

Monica stifled a gasp. She had heard enough. Mick must have married Jolie because his visa had run out. It had never occurred to her to check his status when she'd hired him. Gus had vouched for him and she'd taken his word for it. So far, he'd been a stellar employee and she admitted to herself she hadn't wanted to ask too many questions.

But now it sounded as if he was planning on leaving to work somewhere else. Not that she could blame him. La Nourriture would certainly be a step up from a job baking for Sassamanash Farm.

She didn't want him to catch her and realize she had overheard his conversation. She released the brake on Teddy's carriage and begin to wheel it toward the door. The wheels squeaked and she cringed. Had Mick heard? She risked a glance at the door to the storage room but there was no sign of him.

If only she could get out the door without making any noise. She was almost there when the edge of the carriage bumped the table. She glanced at Teddy but he was still asleep, although he had begun to move restlessly. It wouldn't be long before he woke up with a loud wail.

Finally, she reached the door, pulled it open and eased the carriage over the threshold. She didn't breathe until she and Teddy were outside and on the path toward home.

She didn't know what she'd do if Mick left the farm kitchen now. Her chest felt tight and she drew a panicky breath. It would mean cutting her maternity leave short because she'd never be able to find a baker on such short notice. It had taken months to find Janice. Mick's arrival had been sheer good fortune and probably wouldn't be repeated.

She had another thought that nearly caused her to stumble over a tree root that had grown onto the path. If Mick married Jolie to get a green card, and he no longer needed her, it gave him a good motive for murder.

Especially if Jolie had money. Monica remembered her diamond stud earrings.

She was going to have to find out more, because it wouldn't be long before Detective Stevens came to the same conclusion and would be knocking on Mick's door. He needed to be prepared.

• • •

Monica had grown up eating Sunday dinner. No pizza or takeout—her mother would make a roast chicken with all the trimmings or shepherd's pie with homemade mashed potatoes. It was a habit she found hard to break. She'd gone to Bart's Butcher Shop on Friday and picked up a piece of beef to make Greg a pot roast. She'd cook some carrots and potatoes along with it. It was the perfect dinner for an early fall evening that was beginning to turn brisk.

She opened the refrigerator and Hercule was instantly by her side, making his most persuasive face.

"This isn't for dogs," Monica said. She put the roast in the Dutch oven sitting on the stove. "But I'm sure we can spare a morsel or two after it's cooked."

Mittens seemed drawn by the roast as well and wound in and out between Monica's legs.

She'd fed Teddy and put him down for his nap and was peeling carrots when there was a knock on the back door.

Hercule's ears perked up and he turned his head from side to side as if he was thinking—is this friend or foe?

"Come in," Monica yelled.

"Hello, hello." Gina burst into the room with the force of a hurricane. "Got anything to drink?" She reached down to scratch Hercule's ears.

"You know where it is." Monica motioned toward one of the cabinets with her head. She knew from experience Gina wasn't talking about a glass of water or some iced tea.

Gina got out the bottle of whiskey and a glass and poured herself a shot.

"Do you want some ice? Water?"

"This is fine." Gina held the glass to her mouth and tilted it back. "I needed that."

"Why? What's up?"

"Oh. Nothing really." Gina plopped into a chair at the kitchen table and began fiddling with the buttons on her blouse. "Mickey's mother is coming to meet me." She made a face. "She's flying in from Florida. He says not to worry, she's going to love me." She looked down at herself. "Do I look okay?"

Monica took in Gina's outfit, zebra-print pants, black silk blouse with a deep V-neck, stiletto ankle boots and huge gold hoops with crystals dangling from them.

Monica gulped. "Like Mickey said, I'm sure she's going to love you."

Gina's expression was grim. "I hope Jeff and Lauren don't hear about Jolie's murder. What a terrible thing to happen. I feel responsible."

"Don't be ridiculous." Monica cut the last carrot into chunks and dropped them in the pot, nestling them around the roast. "How could you possibly be responsible?"

"Mick asked me if he could bring his new wife to the wedding. I said okay. I wish I hadn't. Then this would never have happened."

Gina got up and poured another shot of whiskey into her glass. "I wonder who killed the poor woman?"

"I'm sure the police will find out in due time." Monica finished peeling and cutting the potatoes and added them to the pot on the stove.

Gina gave a harsh laugh. "That poor guy from the porta-potty place must have gotten the shock of his life."

"I imagine he did. Although he mostly seemed concerned about returning the porta-potties. He'd waited long enough to pick them up."

Monica paused with the pot lid in her hand. "What do you mean?"

"His truck was parked just beyond your cottage right before we sat down to eat. I'd left my phone in your kitchen and wanted to take some pictures. I saw him then." Gina ran her finger around the rim of her glass. "I saw him again when I went back to your place to use the powder room." She made a face. "I'm afraid I can't stand those porta-potties."

"What was he doing?"

"The second time he was talking to some girl."

"A guest? Who was it? What did she look like?"

Gina shrugged. "She was leaning in the driver's window of his truck. I couldn't see her face." She pointed her finger at Monica. "I did notice she had blond hair though."

Monica raised her eyebrows. "Half the women at the reception had blond hair. I wonder if she was a guest . . . or someone else?"

"She had fancy earrings on. My guess is that she was a guest getting cozy with Mr. Johnny-on-the-Spot." She glanced at Monica out of the corner of her eye. "I have to admit he was kind of cute."

"Was the woman his age? He seemed young."

Gina furrowed her brow. "I couldn't tell. Not from that distance.

She might have been."

Monica thought about it as she turned on the burner under the pot roast. It might mean something and it might mean nothing at all. But surely the young man had other deliveries to make or porta-potties to return to Johnny-on-the-Spot.

It wouldn't be the first time an employee had slacked off on the job. Maybe the woman was his girlfriend and they'd decided to sneak a few moments together away from prying eyes.

Monica's shoulders relaxed. That was probably it and there was no need to bother Stevens with the information. She had enough to do without being sent down rabbit holes that led nowhere.

• • •

Monica tried to persuade Gina to stay for dinner but she said Mickey was taking the night off and they were going to make dinner together, which Monica knew meant that Mickey was going to cook while Gina nursed a martini and watched.

Greg was in the living room. The jingle announcing the local news had just come on when Greg called out, "Monica. Come see this."

Monica wiped her hands on her apron and dashed into the living room. "What is it?"

Greg pointed at the television. "Look. They're talking about Sassamanash Farm."

Monica perched on the edge of the ottoman and turned her attention to the screen, where a young blond reporter was standing in front of the porta-potty that was still down by the bogs. She was smiling brightly and hugging a microphone to her chest.

"Jack," she said, speaking to the news anchor, "I'm at Sassamanash Farm, a cranberry farm here in Cranberry Cove, where the police believe a murder took place sometime on Saturday evening."

The camera focused on the crime scene tape encircling the scene, which obligingly made an ominous snapping sound as the wind whipped it back and forth.

The wind also blew the reporter's hair across her face and she brushed it away impatiently. "A young woman was murdered right here." She pointed to the porta-potty again.

Monica thought calling Jolie young was going a bit too far but she supposed it made her a more sympathetic victim. It reminded her of when newspapers called all younger women coeds whether they were or not.

"Police believe she was suffocated and then placed inside this very porta-potty, which had been rented for a wedding being held right here on the farm. The killer has not yet been identified. The police don't believe it was a random killing but that the killer and victim knew each other, so there is no need for panic. Stay tuned to WZZZ for further details when they are released." She smiled at the camera. "Back to you, Jack."

"How about that?" Greg said. "The farm has made the evening news."

"Not exactly the publicity we wanted."

"What is that saying? There's no such thing as bad publicity."

"Just so we don't have tour buses stopping here to see the grisly site."

"I wouldn't worry about that." Greg stood up. "Is that roast almost ready? The smell is making my mouth water."

• • •

Greg left for Book 'Em early on Monday morning. Monica was already up feeding Teddy in the nursery. Hercule was curled into a circle on the rug, his head on his paws, and Mittens was stretched out in the sunbeam coming through the window.

"Okay, Hercule, let's go," Monica said when Teddy was finished.

Hercule leapt to his feet and wagged his tail enthusiastically.

Monica got Teddy into his sweater, put on her own jacket and tucked Teddy into the baby carrier, where he snuggled against her chest. She clipped the leash on Hercule. "Ready to go?"

Hercule's tail wagged even faster as they walked out the door and headed down the path. More leaves had fallen from the trees and Monica scuffed through them, enjoying the sound they made. She'd loved doing that since she was a child and it was something she'd missed when she lived in Chicago.

They passed the spot where Jeff and Lauren had said I do and Monica noticed the police had removed the porta-potty. She was glad it was gone. It was a reminder of what had happened and all she wanted to remember was the joy and beauty of Jeff and Lauren's wedding day.

As she approached the bog, she noticed a crowd of people standing alongside it.

Two of Jeff's crew were waist-deep in the water, maneuvering the boom and corralling the floating berries onto a conveyor belt and into a waiting truck.

Mauricio, who had been working for Jeff for a long time, was standing on the bank of the bog, the straps of his chest-high waders hanging off his shoulders. He walked over to Monica.

"Hey there, boy." He ruffled Hercule's fur. He peered at Teddy, who was now asleep in his carrier. "I swear he gets bigger every time I see him." He gently ran his hand over Teddy's soft, downy head.

"Are all those people here to watch the harvest?" Monica pointed toward the assembled group huddled together in the distance. Lauren used to give tours when the cranberries were being harvested before she graduated college and her marketing business took off.

Mauricio made a disgusted sound. "I heard them talking and apparently they came to see the site where the murder took place." He hooked his thumbs through the straps of his waders. "Awfully ghoulish of them, if you ask me."

"Of course." Monica slapped her forehead. "It was on the news last night. A reporter was standing right by the bog. I wondered if this would happen. People love the macabre. Just so giant tour buses don't start rolling in."

"The publicity might not be all bad."

"That's what Greg said. But I don't see how it could help the farm."

He shrugged. "They have to park by the farm store and walk over here. Maybe they'll pop in and buy something."

"We'll see," Monica said. But she wasn't too hopeful. Most likely the thrill seekers would be more of a nuisance than anything else.

• • •

"You need to get out of the house," Gina said when Monica picked up the phone later that morning.

"But I was at Jeff's wedding. Isn't that *out*?"

Gina ignored her. "Let's go to lunch. Just the two of us. It will give you a chance to put on some nice clothes, do your hair and makeup."

Did she look that bad? Monica wondered. Her usual outfit consisted of jeans and a T-shirt or sweater depending on the weather, but she *had* dressed up for Jeff's wedding.

"I'll have to bring Teddy."

"Bah. Let that woman who works for Greg at the bookstore watch him for an hour."

"Wilma? But she's supposed to be helping Greg."

"Surely he can manage on his own for a bit."

In the end, Monica agreed to go to lunch. It was impossible to argue with Gina, mainly because she didn't listen. She kept an ear cocked for Teddy, who was napping in his crib while she put on some lipstick and ran a brush through her hair. She didn't have many choices in the way of clothes—her body hadn't gone back to normal yet—but she did have a pair of black pants and a silk blouse that she hoped would do the trick.

She had to admit it did feel rather good to put on some nice clothes and fix herself up. She changed Teddy, who had woken up, and put him in a new outfit her mother had given him. She thought they looked quite the pair.

They'd agreed to meet at the Pepper Pot, where Gina's husband always reserved a table for her and her friends. Monica buckled Teddy into his car seat and put a light blanket over his lap, and he kicked and reached out, trying to grab her hair.

Monica paused for a moment to watch him smiling and gurgling then got into the driver's seat and started the car.

Monica was tempted to stop the car and admire the view at the top of the rise leading into town, but a patrol car was stationed there, obviously waiting to snag speeders. Lake Michigan was visible in the distance as she began down the hill into town. The sun shimmered off the water and the waves were calm and lightly crested with foam. A couple was walking hand in hand at the edge of the beach, their pant legs rolled up and the water lapping at their ankles. As Monica drove down Beach Hollow Road, she noticed a number of tourists walking along, swinging shopping bags and peering into the store windows. Once the leaves fell from the trees, Cranberry Cove would be quiet again. The residents would be glad to see the crowds go, although they did appreciate the boost in the economy that summer brought.

Monica found a parking spot halfway between the Pepper Pot and Book 'Em. She bundled Teddy into his carriage and wheeled him down to Greg's store.

As Gina had predicted, Wilma was only too happy to look after him for an hour.

"Gina convinced me that I needed a girls' lunch," Monica said as she kissed Greg on the cheek.

Greg smiled indulgently. "Have a good time."

Monica gave a last backward glance at Teddy then quickly left the store before she could change her mind. Someone in a red Porsche with the top down sped down the road, its engine roaring. Monica stepped back on the sidewalk as heads swiveled in its direction. She heard several people muttering under their breath as she crossed the street.

The loud buzz of voices, sounding like so many bees, greeted her when she opened the door to the Pepper Pot. It took a moment for her eyes to adjust to the dimmer light as she scanned the room for Gina. She spotted her in the back and began to walk to the table.

Gina jumped up from her seat and greeted Monica with an air kiss on each cheek.

"Don't you feel better getting out for a bit?"

"I have to admit you were right. I do." She pulled out the chair opposite Gina and sat down. The air was fragrant with the mouth-watering scents of garlic and herbs and it made her stomach growl.

Monica picked up the menu the hostess had handed her and began to scan it. Everything sounded delicious.

"Welcome, ladies." Gina's husband, Mickey, came up to their table. He leaned closer and said in a low voice, "The special today is butternut squash soup with candied pecans. It's going fast so I saved you some if you're interested."

"Sounds good." Monica put her menu down. "I'll have that and the house salad."

Gina looked up from perusing the menu. "I think I'll have the same."

Mickey nodded, tucked the menus under his arm and headed for the swinging door to the kitchen.

Monica looked around the room. A couple was seated at the table next to them. The man kept peeling back his shirt cuff to glance at his watch—a gold Rolodex. Monica assumed he must be on his lunch hour, although with his fancy watch, well-tailored suit and silk tie, she doubted he was the type who had to punch a clock. More likely he had a meeting scheduled with an important client and didn't want to be late.

The silence between the two of them appeared strained. The woman's mouth was turned down and she picked at her food. An expensive Gucci handbag was tucked up next to her chair and her ring finger sparkled with diamonds.

A waitress swept by their table, a tray laden with steaming dishes balanced on her shoulder. Monica caught a whiff of caramelized onions and freshly baked bread.

She set it down on a tray stand and placed bowls of soup and plates of salad on the table in front of Gina and Monica.

Gina glanced after the waitress and leaned forward, nearly dunking the tie on her blouse into her soup. "You know, one of Micky's employees borrowed money from him."

Monica put down her spoon. "That's so kind of him."

"Too kind. Now he's worried they won't pay back the loan."

They continued to chat as they downed their soup and polished off their salads.

The waitress stopped by their table. "Dessert?"

Monica glanced at her watch. She'd probably left Teddy with Wilma long enough.

"No, thanks." She put her napkin on the table. "I should be going. Teddy will be hungry. This was a great idea. Thank you for thinking of it." She kissed Gina on the cheek.

She was walking toward the door when she decided she'd better make a detour to the ladies' room.

The bathroom was small but the designer had managed to make it look warm and cozy. An antique dresser had been repurposed into a vanity with two sinks and a gold-framed mirror hanging above it. One wall was covered in framed illustrations from old cookbooks. Monica recognized a page from her grandmother's *Good Housekeeping* cookbook—a vivid color picture of different kinds of pies.

A woman was in front of the mirror. Monica recognized her as the woman who had been sitting at the table next to her. She pulled a lipstick from her cosmetic bag and leaned closer as she began to carefully fill in her lips. She appeared to be talking to someone in the occupied stall.

Monica entered the unoccupied one and latched the door behind her.

"I think she did it," the woman at the mirror said.

Monica froze. *Who did what?*

"Jolie?" the woman in the stall next to her responded.

Jolie? Monica's ears perked up. *What had she done?* She held her breath as she listened to the conversation.

"It would have been easy enough for her to slip him a bit of extra morphine to ease his pain," The last words were said sarcastically. "Not to mention ushering him swiftly out of this world. Who would know? Certainly, it couldn't be proven." She pulled a brush from her purse and began to fix her hair.

"She wanted the money," the woman in the stall said. "And she wasn't willing to wait. The doctor had given him what? Six months? And it had been eight months already."

"Who marries someone practically on their death bed?"

"The money is the only reason she married him." Monica heard the click of the latch on the stall door. "Look at those earrings Father gave her as a wedding present." Her voice was bitter. "Those were Mother's favorites. They should have gone to one of us. She probably couldn't wait to dip into the rest of the Spencer jewels."

"Not to mention the bank accounts." Monica heard the woman at the mirror snap her purse shut.

"And Father was barely cold in his grave when she turned around and married that gigolo."

Monica let her breath out in a rush. Were they talking about Jolie's late husband? And were they insinuating that Jolie . . .

The woman exited the stall at the same time as Monica. They both headed toward the sinks. Monica glanced at the woman's reflection in the mirror. She was surprised to see the other woman was the server from Jeff and Lauren's wedding. She thought her name was Heather.

Why were they talking about Jolie? They were clearly the daughters of her late husband.

"Let's just hope Father did what we told him to," Heather said.

The other woman laughed. "If he did, that young man she married is in for a big surprise."

Chapter 4

Teddy was in his baby swing contentedly examining his hands and putting his fingers in his mouth while Monica finished packing a carton. Hercule wandered over and poked his nose in the box, found nothing of interest and went to curl up on his dog bed.

"Another one done," she said to Greg, who was filling a box with books.

Their new house was nearly ready and Monica didn't want to wait until the last minute to pack. The task was overwhelming enough as it was.

She sat back on her heels and looked around the living room. "Suddenly I'm feeling all nostalgic about this cottage." She dabbed at her eyes with the edge of her T-shirt.

"A lot of happy times here." Greg smiled at her. "But we'll have more room in the new house, which we'll need as Teddy gets older." He squeezed her shoulder. "And we'll make new memories there that will be just as wonderful."

"That's true. By the way, I overheard an interesting conversation today." Monica ripped a piece of packing tape from the roll. "Two women. I recognized one of them. She was part of the waitstaff at Jeff and Lauren's wedding. Her name is Heather. I don't know who the other woman was but it seemed clear they were related. They obviously thought that Jolie had hastened her late husband's death by giving him an extra dose of morphine."

Greg whistled. "That's quite an accusation. How would she have gotten hold of morphine? You can't simply walk into a pharmacy and grab some off the shelf."

"I don't know. I suppose he'd been prescribed morphine by his doctor. It sounded as if the doctors didn't expect him to live much longer."

"In that case, he was probably receiving hospice care. I suppose they're able to administer morphine."

"Oh!"

Greg lowered his brows and tilted his head to one side. "What is it?"

"Maybe Jolie worked for the hospice company. One of those home health aides or something. And that's how she met her husband."

Greg shrugged. "It's possible."

Monica was about to begin filling another carton when her phone rang. She pulled it out of the pocket of her jeans and answered the call.

"Monica, it's Mom."

Monica looked at Greg and rolled her eyes. "I know."

There was a moment of silence, then Nancy continued. "The strangest thing happened. It was in the middle of the night last night. I was sound asleep when I heard a loud thud. I was going to investigate but there were no further noises. I thought I must have dreamt it. Besides, I'd forgotten to close the bedroom window and it was chilly. I didn't feel like getting out from under the covers."

Where was this going? Monica wondered.

"Did you figure out what it was?"

"You know that clock that's on my mantelpiece? The one my godmother gave me? When I got up this morning and went into the living room, I found it on the floor, sadly in pieces."

"That's too bad." The clock had been on the mantel in their old house as far back as Monica could remember.

"Well, what could have happened?" Her mother sounded indignant. "What made it fall? It was hardly in a precarious position."

"I don't know." Monica glanced at Mittens, who was known to occasionally swipe things off tabletops. "You don't have a cat."

"Do you think it was a ghost?"

Monica laughed. "You're joking. Aren't you?"

"It's not funny. This is serious."

"But a ghost? Surely you don't believe in them."

"I don't know. There was that program on television that time . . ."

"It's more likely something jostled the house slightly. A large truck going by or . . . or something. I wouldn't worry about it. It probably won't happen again."

Nancy sighed. "I suppose you're right, dear."

Greg raised his eyebrows as Monica ended the call. "Your mother?"

"Yes. She seems to think a ghost knocked that large clock off her mantelpiece in the middle of the night."

Greg frowned. "Your mother is getting on in years. Perhaps one of those retirement communities would be a good idea. There's that new one . . . what's it called?"

"Sunset Living?" Monica snorted. "She's not that old. Besides, you'd never convince her to do that." She ripped another piece of tape from the roll. She was about to fasten the box when she paused. "It is strange though. She's never been the fanciful type. I can't imagine she really believes in ghosts."

Greg looked at her and frowned. "Let's hope not."

• • •

Monica was in the kitchen the next morning cleaning away the breakfast things but her mind was elsewhere. She couldn't stop thinking about the conversation she'd heard in the ladies' room at the Pepper Pot. Had Jolie worked for the hospice company taking care of her late husband? Mick might know but she wasn't ready to face him yet—not after learning he was considering an offer from a restaurant in Chicago. She wasn't known for her poker face. She was afraid she'd slip and reveal that she'd overheard his conversation. Presumably, he'd tell her soon enough if he planned to leave the farm. But how else could she find out about Jolie's past?

Teddy had fallen asleep in his baby seat, his head lolling to one side, a bit of drool escaping from the corner of his mouth. Monica retrieved her laptop, put it on the kitchen table and powered it up.

A quick search revealed there was a hospice serving the Cranberry Cove area—the Loving Hands Hospice. Monica let out a breath. Did she dare call them?

She slammed her laptop shut in frustration. What was she doing? It wasn't her job to figure out who had killed Jolie. Detective Stevens was perfectly capable of doing it all by herself.

She busied herself with tasks around the house. She picked up the newspaper they'd left scattered around the living room, plumped the sofa cushions, did a load of laundry, but she still couldn't get her mind off the idea that Jolie might have been a nurse or home health aide working for the hospice that took care of her husband.

By noon, her curiosity had gotten the better of her. She couldn't stand it any longer. Teddy had been fed and was down for his nap, it was the perfect time to act.

She powered up her computer again and searched for Loving Hands Hospice. She jotted down the number and pulled out her cell phone. It rang and rang on the other end and she was about to give up when someone answered.

A woman with a high-pitched voice said in soothing tones, "Loving Hands Hospice. You're in good hands with Loving Hands. How may I help you?"

Monica hesitated. She cleared her throat but her voice still came out in a nervous rasp.

"Can I speak to Jolie Spencer, please? She's a nurse there." As soon as she said it, she realized Jolie would have had a different last name at the time. But Jolie was an unusual first name. Maybe the receptionist would put two and two together.

"Let me see." There was a pause. "We don't seem to have a Jolie Spencer working here."

Monica was disappointed, but it was nothing more than she had expected.

"But," the woman said brightly, "we used to have a Jolie Clawson. Jolie's an unusual name, isn't it? She told us it means pretty in French." Her tone was gossipy. "But she wasn't a nurse. She was a home health aide. There's quite a difference. The training's different and so is the job."

Monica heard someone say something in the background.

"Excuse me. I won't be a minute."

The sound became muffled and she assumed the woman had put her hand over the mouthpiece.

"Sorry about that." The voice came over the line again. "I heard Jolie got married so Spencer must be her new married name." Her tone became conspiratorial. "Denise, she's the administrative assistant here, said she met her husband on the job. I can't even imagine." She paused. "Anyway, can someone else help you? Are you looking for a home health aide? Because Flo is great. All our clients love her."

"Actually, I needed to speak to Jolie about something else. We'd lost touch and I wanted to catch up. But thank you for your help. Goodbye."

Monica ended the call before the receptionist could ask any more questions. She flopped against the back of her chair. She'd gotten something from the phone call at least. More than she'd expected.

Way more. It wasn't a leap to conclude that the man Jolie had met and married on the job was her patient—that Spencer fellow.

Maybe Heather and that other woman were right. Jolie had married him knowing he was dying. It sounded as if there was money involved and wouldn't she, as his wife, be the one to inherit?

Did Mick stand to get the money now that Jolie was dead? Dread crept into the pit of Monica's stomach. That would give Mick an even stronger motive for killing Jolie.

How much longer before Detective Stevens came to the same conclusion?

Was she going to lose Mick to an upscale restaurant in Chicago, or was she going to lose him to . . . jail?

Chapter 5

Monica had just finished feeding Teddy when Gina walked in brandishing a piece of paper. It looked like an invoice.

"I'm so steamed," she said, blowing a lock of hair off her face.

"What's wrong?" Monica kept her voice level. Gina was capable of being equally steamed over a massive problem or something completely trivial.

"It's that porta-potty company Johnny-on-the-Spot. They charged me for four porta-potties when we only asked for three and that's all they delivered." She slammed the paper down on the table. "I tried calling them but I got absolutely nowhere. I thought maybe you'd have better luck."

"Me?" Monica pointed at herself. "I'm not sure I can do anything."

"I thought maybe if you went over there and talked to the manager . . ."

"Me?" Monica said again. She gestured toward Teddy, who appeared to be watching the entire conversation from his baby seat.

"I'll stay with Teddy." Gina made little goo-goo noises at him and chucked him under the chin. "What's-her-name is minding the shop for me."

Gina had had so many assistants since she opened Making Scents, her aromatherapy shop, that Monica couldn't keep track of them. Obviously neither could Gina. It was as if the store had a revolving door sucking them in and spitting them out one after the other.

Monica was about to refuse when she realized this was an opportunity to find out more about Timmy, the young man who had delivered the porta-potties. Why had he been hanging around the farm before picking them up? Had he known Jolie? Maybe someone at Johnny-on-the-Spot would know the answer.

"Fine. I've just changed and fed Teddy so he should be good for a while. If he gets fussy, his pacifiers are in the dish drainer by the sink." Monica grabbed the invoice off the table and glanced at it quickly. It was straightforward enough.

She slung her purse over her shoulder and reached for the handle to the back door. "I'll try to be quick."

"Don't worry about us. We'll be fine. Won't we, Teddy," Gina said in a baby voice.

Monica headed to her car. She'd been planning to go to the farm kitchen to see how things were going but she'd have to put that on hold until later.

The air was fresh and she buzzed down her windows, letting the breeze in. She'd looked up Johnny-on-the-Spot and it was on the other side of the harbor beyond the town center. She glanced to her left as she neared the harbor and the Cranberry Cove Yacht Club. In the distance, sailboats glided across the lake, their sails flapping and billowing in the brisk wind.

The route ultimately took her down a rather shabby street with dilapidated buildings and a seedy bar whose door was propped open, the sound of voices and the smell of beer drifting through Monica's open window. It was the sort of place that attracted customers wanting a drink to get them going in the morning and a couple to ease them to sleep at night.

The street led to a small industrial park housing several businesses, including Johnny-on-the-Spot. It was on the end and a large enclosed lot dotted with porta-potties lined up in rows was next to it.

The smell of disinfectant hit Monica the minute she opened the door to the office. Several dented metal desks were arranged around the space. The linoleum floor was cracked and yellowed in spots and the walls could have used a coat of paint.

A woman was sitting at the desk in front, her head partially hidden by her computer monitor. A drooping philodendron was perched on one corner of the desk and several faded greeting cards were arranged along the edge.

Monica cleared her throat and the woman peered around the edge of her monitor. Her eyelids drooped and there were dark circles underneath. She had a stain on her blouse that Monica recognized from experience was baby spit-up. She lifted a hand and let it flop down again. Monica felt a wave of sympathy for her.

"Can I help you?" Her voice was hoarse with weariness.

Monica dug the invoice out of her purse. "There seems to be some mistake with this bill. Is there someone I can talk to?"

She swiveled her chair around and yelled through the open door to the office beyond. "Hey, Lou. Customer needs you."

She waited several beats before shrugging. "Guess he's not in. Can you come back another time?"

"Sure."

The woman turned back to her computer monitor and began typing.

Monica was about to reach for the door to leave when it opened and a man walked in.

The woman popped her head out rather like a prairie dog emerging from its burrow. "Hey, Lou. This lady needs help. Something about the bill."

"Sure." Lou smiled at Monica and indicated for her to follow him.

He was a short, squat man with salt-and-pepper hair that was cut close to the scalp and stood up like the bristles on a hairbrush.

He led Monica into a small office crowded with an old wooden desk and several gunmetal gray filing cabinets. A fan, its blades coated with dust, stood in the corner.

Lou perched on the edge of the desk. "So what can I do for you?"

Monica handed him the invoice. "We only ordered three porta-potties but were charged for four."

Lou frowned and glanced at the paper in his hand. He flicked it with a finger. "It says here four were delivered."

Monica took a steadying breath. "We only received the three we ordered."

"Hey, Steph. Can you check"—he glanced at the paper—"the Albertson order and see how many potties were returned to the yard on Saturday?"

Monica wet her lips. "By the way, your young man did an excellent job. He was very polite and very helpful."

"Timmy? Yeah, I'm glad I hired him. I had my doubts. I don't normally hire convicted felons, you know, but I decided to give him a chance. I'm glad I did. He's doing a good job." He jerked his thumb toward the office door. "Better than some of the others." He shook his head.

Stephanie stuck her head in the door. "Two potties were returned on Saturday." She glanced back at her computer. "And one this morning."

For a moment Lou looked puzzled but then his face cleared. "That's right. The police were holding on to one of them." He whistled. "Poor kid had the shock of his life when that body fell out. I feel sorry for him. Have the police figured out what happened yet?

Did she have a heart attack while sitting on the john?" He chuckled.

Monica decided it was best to feign ignorance. "I don't know. I expect it will be on the news any day now."

Lou rubbed his chin. "But that doesn't explain what happened to the fourth porta-potty."

"There was no fourth. Like I told you, we only received three."

"I'm going to have to look into that. Steph!" he yelled through the open door. "Remind me to check on that fourth porta-potty. And prepare another invoice for Albertson for three porta-potties, not the four we originally billed them for."

"Sorry about that," he said, putting the invoice on his desk, where it joined an untidy stack of papers.

Gina would be pleased, Monica thought, as she pulled out of the parking lot of Johnny-on-the-Spot. She'd succeeded in convincing them to correct the bill. But she'd achieved something else as well. She now knew Timmy had been in jail and had a criminal record. She wasn't sure how, or if, that tied him into Jolie's murder. But it certainly made his behavior suspicious. She wondered what he'd been in jail for and would have asked Lou but she hadn't wanted to display too much interest in Timmy. He might begin to question her motives. No doubt it would be easy enough to find out some other way.

The case of the missing porta-potty—she had to laugh—was curious. It sounded like a Sherlock Holmes story. Was it tied to Jolie's murder in any way?

She was confident she would eventually find out.

• • •

Monica glanced at the clock on the car's dashboard. It was nearly time to feed Teddy. The timing had been perfect. There was little traffic on the road and Monica sailed along until she ended up behind a massive cement mixer that looked like an elephant lumbering down the street. She tapped the steering wheel impatiently as she watched the minutes tick by. Finally, the truck pulled off onto a side street and she was able to move at a pace brisker than a crawl.

The traffic light ahead of her was green, but as she approached it, it turned yellow, and just as she reached it, it turned red. Monica slammed on the brakes. She looked around as she waited. She was right in front of the dive bar she'd passed earlier. The sign over the door was faded but she could make out the name—the Harborside Lounge Bar and Grill. Monica laughed. That almost made it sound upscale. The fact that it was a bar and grill was evident from the smell of spilled beer mingling with the odor of overdone burgers drifting out the door.

Movement at the entrance caught her eye and she turned to look. A man walked out holding a blond woman by the arm. She tripped as he yanked her over the threshold. He was a rough-looking character with crude tattoos snaking up both arms.

The blond looked familiar even though Monica couldn't see all of her face. The man had his back to the street as the blond shook free from his grasp and turned toward him.

Monica squinted. It was Heather, the server from the Pepper Pot. What was she doing in a disreputable bar like the Harborside Lounge? And with a man who looked like a gangster?

The man brought his face close to Heather's and she stumbled back a step. He took her arm again and shook her.

Was she in trouble? Monica looked around but there wasn't much she could do. There was nowhere to park and besides, she doubted she'd be much of a match for that man, whose biceps bulged beneath the short sleeves of his T-shirt.

A horn honked, startling her. She checked her rearview mirror and saw the driver behind her pointing at the light. She looked up. It was green. With a wave of apology, she stepped on the gas.

She glanced in her rearview mirror again as she drove off. Heather was walking down the street, away from the man she'd been talking to. She seemed okay. Monica breathed a sigh of relief.

• • •

Jolie's memorial service was being held at the Restful Haven funeral parlor. Monica hadn't known Jolie but she felt it was important to support Mick.

She bundled Teddy into his car seat and headed out. She reflexively slowed as she approached the crest of the hill into town. As she had suspected, the Cranberry Cove patrol car was parked in the shadows alongside the road.

She continued down Beach Hollow Road, past the shops, until she came to Sandy Lane, a small side street tucked behind the library and near the Episcopal church. The road was overhung with trees and the gutters were overflowing with red and gold leaves.

Monica pulled into the parking lot, relieved to see that some cars were already there. She retrieved Teddy's carriage from the trunk and opened it next to the back door of the car. Teddy had been dozing but his eyes opened briefly as she buckled him in before he drifted back to sleep.

Restful Haven was located in an old Victorian house with a steep gabled roof painted pea soup green. The winding brick path leading to the door was strewn with leaves that crunched under the wheels of Teddy's carriage.

An arched portico shaded the large front door. Monica spied what appeared to be an old-fashioned bell pull along with a highly polished brass door knocker in the shape of a pineapple. She turned the handle and the door opened into an expansive foyer with a wooden floor overlaid with a jewel-toned Oriental carpet.

A gentleman in a black suit and black tie glided toward her, his hands clasped as if in prayer. His voice was soft and mellow and Monica felt as if it flowed over her.

"May I help you?" His expression was sympathetic.

"I'm here for the memorial for Jolie Amentas."

"Right this way, please." He ushered her down a long hall with various rooms opening off of it and led her into a spacious room at the end. It had high ceilings with ornate molding and tall windows letting in a shaft of sunlight. A casket stood at the front with rows of chairs lined up behind it. A small knot of people was standing at the back of the room chatting in low voices. One of the women was wearing a pair of light blue scrubs.

Monica looked around for Mick. She didn't see him at first but then spied him talking to the man in the black suit and tie. Monica waited until they had finished before approaching Mick. She planned to keep the conversation brief. She still felt awkward about the fact that she knew that Mick was possibly planning on leaving Sassamanash Farm.

"Mick. I don't know what to say. I can't tell you how sorry I am for your loss."

Mick bowed his head briefly. "Thank you. That means a lot to me."

"I didn't realize you'd gotten married." Monica tried to keep the accusatory tone out of her voice. Part of her felt guilty for not getting to know Mick better.

"It was a spur-of-the-moment decision. We already knew we wanted to spend our lives together. Why wait?" He glanced at the coffin. "We had no idea our time was going to be so short."

"How did you and Jolie meet?" Monica assumed they ran in two rather different circles.

"Jolie had a flat tire. I stopped to help her and I guess you'd say we just hit it off. We went for a drink and that was it. Like I said, we didn't see any point in waiting."

Had they really hit it off, Monica wondered, or had Mick seen a golden opportunity—a green card and a fortune all in one swoop?

"Excuse me," Mick said to Monica. "I must go say hello." He gestured toward the door, where a man in jeans and a sweatshirt was standing.

Monica debated leaving. She'd done her duty. That was enough, wasn't it?

She was about to wheel Teddy to the door when two women walked in. Monica nearly gasped. It was Heather and the woman she'd been talking to in the ladies' room at the Pepper Pot. Why had they come? They were obviously hardly fans of Jolie.

A woman appeared at Monica's elbow. "How long had you known Jolie?" She was the one Monica had noticed earlier, the one in scrubs.

"I only met her on Saturday. She is . . . was married to one of my employees."

"The new husband?"

"Yes."

Monica noticed Heather and her companion approach the casket.

"I'm Flo, by the way. Jolie and I worked together." She tipped her head toward the coffin. "I don't know what those two are doing here. They hated Jolie and made her life miserable." She gave a bitter laugh. "Perhaps they want to verify that Jolie is well and truly dead."

"Who are they?" Monica said. "I know the one—Heather—is Jolie's stepdaughter."

"The other one is her sister Courtney." Flo's lips tightened. "Jolie was their father's home health aide through Loving Hands." She tucked a strand of hair behind her ear. "Heather was bad enough, constantly telling Jolie her father must have been delusional when he married her and reminding her she'd been nothing but a home health aide and not to put on airs now that she was Mrs. Richard Spencer." Her lips tightened further. "But Courtney!" She nodded her head in Courtney's direction. Do you know what she did?"

Monica shook her head. "No."

"She called Loving Hands Hospice. That's where Jolie was working when she was assigned to the Spencer case. She told our manager that she suspected Jolie had injected their father with a fatal overdose of morphine." She snorted. "They couldn't accept that it was simply his time. She wanted to call the police. Poor Jolie was terrified she was going to be arrested for something she hadn't done. How would she be able to prove it?"

Monica looked in Heather and Courtney's direction again. Had Courtney really believed that Jolie had murdered her father?

Both Heather and Courtney knew their father was dying. There was no doubt about that even though no one knew the timing. Had they been so devoted to him or was it something else? Were they getting impatient waiting for the money, which to their disappointment was left solely to Jolie, their stepmother?

Chapter 6

The service for Jolie was short and simple, led by the man who had greeted Monica at the door to the funeral parlor. He read a poem by Henry Scott-Holland, "Death Is Nothing at All," then motioned to a man who had been standing by the casket.

He introduced himself as Jolie's brother. He was wearing a dusty-looking black suit that was showing its age and a white shirt with a limp collar. He fumbled in his pocket and pulled out a much-creased piece of paper. He unfolded it, glanced at it and began a brief eulogy saying that he and Jolie hadn't seen much of each other since they'd grown up but he had fond memories of their childhood together.

He said a few more words, bowed his head, then collapsed into an empty chair in the first row.

A young woman who had been sitting next to Jolie's brother got up and walked to the lectern. She was wearing a black dress that even Monica knew was no longer in style. It must have been purchased for a previous funeral and been hanging in her closet waiting for the next one.

Monica didn't know her but she looked familiar. She turned her head and her gold hoop earrings swayed against her neck. Monica had a flash back to Jeff and Lauren's wedding and the woman who had been arguing with Jolie right before Jolie headed toward the porta-potties.

She sniffed, pulled a tissue from her pocket and wiped her eyes. "I'm Candi Clawson, Jolie's daughter. My mother . . ." she began.

Her eulogy was over in under five minutes. Teddy was starting to fuss and Monica felt as if she'd done more than her due as far as Jolie was concerned. She began wheeling his carriage toward the door.

Heather and Courtney were in a knot by the door talking in low tones. Teddy's blanket slipped off of him and landed on the floor. As Monica bent to retrieve it, she heard part of Heather and Courtney's conversation.

"I won't have anywhere to go." Heather sounded near tears.

"It's your own fault."

"I told the landlord I'd have the money soon but he still sent me an eviction notice. It's not fair." She pulled a tissue from her pocket and wiped her eyes. "Can you help me? Please?"

"I'm afraid I can't."

Monica had finished arranging Teddy's blanket and had no excuse to linger any longer. How frustrating! It sounded as if Heather was in dire financial straits and for some reason, her sister wouldn't help her out. She thought back to her lunch with Gina and the expensive bag Courtney was carrying and her husband's Rolex watch. It certainly looked as if she had the wherewithal to loan her sister some money.

Maybe her sister had a history of not repaying loans and Courtney was fed up with it?

Had Heather expected to inherit money when her father died? Did she think getting Jolie out of the way would accomplish that?

Monica really wished she could see Richard Spencer's will. It would answer a lot of questions. She contemplated it as she wheeled Teddy to the car. Maybe she would be able to think of a way.

• • •

Teddy had been fed and was napping while Monica made herself a burrito topped with cranberry salsa. She plunked into a chair at the kitchen table and sighed. She envied Teddy his nap. She could do with one herself. She hadn't expected motherhood to be quite so tiring. Teddy still needed feedings during the night and even though Greg changed his diaper and brought him to her, it still kept her from getting a good night's sleep.

Her head began to droop and she jerked awake. She needed air. That would wake her up. It was the perfect time to walk down to the farm kitchen and check on things. She heard Teddy beginning to stir in his crib. He would probably enjoy being outside as well.

The temperature had dropped, although Monica knew there would still be a few warm days at the end of September and heading into October. She bundled Teddy into one of the handmade sweaters he'd been gifted, pulled on her own fleece and in no time they were out the door.

There was a distinct autumnal chill in the air and it smelled of drying leaves and apples from a nearby orchard. Monica immediately felt refreshed and Teddy began cooing and kicking his feet in his carriage.

She bent to readjust his blanket then continued down the path toward the farm kitchen.

A feeling almost like homesickness washed over her as she pulled open the door and maneuvered the carriage over the threshold. She stopped for a moment to inhale the intoxicating scent of sugar, cranberries and yeast.

She had been hesitant to face Mick, but the feeling vanished as soon as she stepped inside.

The normality of the scene—Mick at the counter cutting out scones, Janice next to him kneading dough and Nancy at the table tying ribbons around jars of cranberry compote—put her at ease. As soon as they saw her, Nancy and Janice immediately deserted their positions to lean over the carriage and admire Teddy.

"He's getting so big. Aren't you my special boy," Nancy said.

Janice frowned. She called to Monica, "Is it windy out?"

Monica raised her eyebrows. "No, not terribly, why?"

"A windy day can give a baby wind," Janice said with an air of satisfaction.

"A baby isn't going to get gas because they've been outside in the wind. That's an old wives' tale."

Janice shook her head. "I don't know. You can't be too careful."

Monica took a steadying breath and smiled. There was no arguing with Janice. She parked the carriage near Nancy and went over to the counter.

"Everything going okay? I feel so guilty not being here to help."

"You need to be with your baby." Janice stuck her hands in the lump of dough on the counter in front of her. "Besides, we're managing just fine." She looked at Mick.

"Yes. No problems." He smiled.

"Good." Monica knocked on the counter. "I'm going to check on our stock."

She strolled around the stockroom but everything was neat and tidy and there were plentiful supplies of everything they would need for the foreseeable future.

Nancy was holding Teddy when Monica reemerged and having a lively conversation with him. He followed her movements with his eyes and tried to grab her hair.

Monica slid into the seat opposite her mother.

Nancy jiggled Teddy. "You know, I'm convinced I have a ghost in the house." Monica opened her mouth but her mother held up a hand. "No matter what you say, I know I'm right."

"Mother, simply because that clock fell off your mantel doesn't mean you have a ghost. Ghosts don't exist. It's your imagination. Something perfectly normal caused it to fall. A truck rumbling by or . . ."

Nancy was already shaking her head. "No. It's true. There's a ghost. That's not the only strange thing that's happened."

"Really?"

"Yes. I left my glasses on the coffee table and when I went to get them, they were gone!" Nancy said triumphantly. "And do you know where I found them?" Before Monica could reply, she continued. "I found them in the pocket of my robe."

"Maybe you put them there and forgot." Monica said it as gently as possible.

Nancy was already shaking her head. "No. I never put them in my robe pocket. That's not all. I was watching the news on television when a cold wind swept through the room—cold enough to make me shiver when I'd been perfectly comfortable a moment before. And yesterday when I walked into the living room, I distinctly smelled a strong perfume in the air. It smelled like gardenia. There's a poltergeist in the house, I tell you."

Meanwhile, Janice had wandered over and was listening to their conversation. "This is the time of year when the veil between the two worlds is at its thinnest." Monica glanced at her but her expression was serious. "No wonder you're hearing ghosts."

"See?" Nancy pointed at Janice. "She believes me."

Monica was about to retort that Janice believed a lot of things that were myths or old wives' tales that had long ago been disproven, but not without some difficulty she managed to hold her tongue.

"It's probably the previous owner haunting the place. Maybe there was some unfinished business at the end of their life or some unresolved trauma." Janice put a hand to her mouth. "Perhaps they were murdered and the killer was never brought to justice. Ghosts have been known to haunt their previous residences in those cases." She frowned. "Do you know who owned the house before you?"

Nancy shook her head. "I'm afraid I don't. It was an estate sale." She grabbed Monica's hand. "Will you check into it? The thought of living in a house where someone was murdered . . ." She shivered.

Monica knew it was useless to argue. Nancy and Janice would hound her until she'd done what Nancy asked. And if it would put her mother's mind at ease and put paid to this whole notion of ghosts, it would be worth it.

"Fine. I'll do it."

• • •

Gina appeared at Monica's door early the next morning. She was wearing leggings, a cropped top and a light zip-up jacket. Monica wasn't sure if that was supposed to be what fashion magazines had taken to calling "athleisure" wear or if Gina was planning to go to the gym later.

Greg's eyebrows rose nearly to his hairline when he saw Gina's attire and he choked on the coffee he was drinking.

"I didn't expect to see you here," Gina said as she took a mug from the cabinet and poured herself coffee. "But I'm glad you are." She nodded at Greg. "Will you be here for a while?"

Greg swallowed his mouthful of coffee. "For a bit, yes. I'm going to an estate sale but it doesn't open until eleven o'clock. Fortunately, the store is busiest in the afternoon so Wilma should be able to handle things by herself."

"Good," Gina said again. "I'm going to borrow your wife." She turned to Monica. "I'm taking you to my exercise class at the Soul Spring Spa." Gina inhaled deeply and threw her hands in the air. "It will release your endorphins and you'll feel wonderful. Kiran is a brilliant teacher."

"What sort of exercise?" Monica was leery.

"I'll tell you about it in the car." She made a shooing motion. "Hurry. Go get changed."

Monica peered at Teddy in his baby seat. He had fallen asleep with his head lolling to one side.

Greg smiled. "Don't worry. I can cope. You go ahead."

Monica dutifully climbed the stairs to their bedroom and rummaged through her drawers. She knew she had an old pair of leggings somewhere left over from when she used to take yoga classes in Chicago. They had a small hole in them but it wasn't that noticeable. She didn't have a fancy top like Gina, and besides, she wanted a bit more coverage. She pulled out an old T-shirt that had faded lettering saying *Monica's Café* on it and wiggled into it. It was a little tight but it would have to do.

She pulled her hair back into a ponytail with an elastic and headed downstairs, where Gina was waiting.

What was she getting herself into, she thought, as she got into the passenger seat of Gina's Mercedes.

"So, tell me about this exercise class we're going to. What do we have to do?"

Monica crossed her fingers that it wouldn't involve things like mountain climbers or jumping jacks or be named something like Boot Camp.

"It's something brand new. It was created in Australia and it's called Zuu."

"Zoo?"

"Yes, but with two u's instead of o's."

A sense of dread crept from Monica's toes to the top of her head. "How do you Zuu?" She laughed. It sounded as if she was saying *how do you do.*

"The exercises are based on animal movements. They're quite natural."

By now they were heading down Beach Hollow Road and within moments Gina was pulling into the parking lot in back of the Soul Spring Spa.

Gina led the way into the facility and motioned toward a wall of cubicles. "You can leave your shoes and purse over there."

"My shoes?"

"Yes. Zuu is performed barefoot. It's more natural and gives you a better grip."

Monica reluctantly yanked off her sneakers, peeled off her socks and stashed them in one of the cubbies.

Gina took her arm. "Over there are the massage rooms, meditation room and sauna."

They passed a towering pyramid of plastic bottles with Thermodynamics in large letters on the label.

Gina pointed at them. "We're going to get you selling those as an ambassador for Soul Spring Spa."

Monica was about to protest, but they'd entered a room with a mirrored wall and yoga mats stacked on one side. Soothing music was being piped in and a diffuser scented the air with lavender.

"Kiran buys his essential oils from me. That's how I met him," Gina said.

Kiran himself sat cross-legged on the floor with his eyes closed and his hands on his knees. He was wearing a dark blue jumpsuit and was barefoot. A bit of light-colored stubble was visible on his head.

Other women had begun to filter into the room and Monica was surprised to see Courtney chatting with a tall blond in leggings patterned in several vivid colors.

Monica looked around, but it was too late to bolt. Besides, she had no way to get back to the farm so she might as well go through with it. How bad could it be?

It wasn't bad, it was worse, Monica decided within the first five minutes. She would have welcomed mountain climbers or jumping jacks instead, when Kiran began to demonstrate the first move—the frog squat. Monica thought that was bad, but then they moved on to the bear crawl. She felt her face getting red and sweat was dripping down her spine. The other women seemed to be having a good time, whooping it up and making animal-like noises.

The minutes ticked by with agonizing slowness but finally the class was over. Kiran headed to a stack of fluffy white towels, all neatly rolled and precisely arranged on a set of shelves. He went around the room and handed them out.

Monica groaned as she dabbed at her face and neck. "That was something," she said to Gina, who appeared to be invigorated and glowing. "No wonder you lost weight."

They began to move toward their cubbies to collect their things. "You should come again," Gina said. She hung her towel around her neck. "It would be good for you."

When pigs fly, Monica muttered to herself. She reached for her shoes and sat on the bench to put them on.

A woman, whose arms and legs revealed the remains of a summer tan, sat next to Monica and began talking to the woman on the other side. Monica glanced at them out of the corner of her eye. The woman's companion was Courtney Spencer.

"They can't do that. You need to get a lawyer. A good one. My friend Daphne used Elizabeth Brennan. She said she was worth every penny. I'll get her contact info for you if you'd like."

Monica had finished tying her sneakers and Gina was waiting for her by the door and she had no choice but to get up.

A cool breeze was blowing and it felt heavenly on her overheated face and neck as she followed Gina out to the car. What did Courtney need a lawyer for? she wondered. It was frustrating not to have heard more of the conversation. Did it have something to do with Richard Spencer's will or was it something else?

Chapter 7

Her phone rang as Monica was pulling into her driveway. She and Teddy had made a quick trip to the farm stand down the road for some sweet potatoes and a head of lettuce for that night's dinner.

She pulled the phone from her purse and quickly peered into the rearview mirror. Another mirror affixed to the backseat allowed her to see Teddy in his backward-facing car seat. His eyes were closed and his mouth was slightly open. It didn't look as if he was going to wake up anytime soon.

Monica swiped her phone open and answered the call. It was Nancy.

"Have you had a chance to look into what we discussed?"

Monica's mind momentarily went blank. "Discussed?"

"Yes. About the ghost in my house and how it might be the previous owner haunting the place. You promised to look into it for me."

Monica stifled a groan. "Of course. Teddy's sleeping so I'll see what I can do now."

"Thank you, dear."

Monica sighed and ended the call. She'd been looking forward to putting her feet up and relaxing for a bit. Instead, she carefully moved Teddy from his car seat to his crib and settled at the kitchen table with her laptop. She did some googling and finally found the property records for her county in Michigan.

She typed in her mother's address and quickly found what she was looking for. The house had previously been owned by an Ada Visser. Monica typed her name into a search engine and links to several Ada Vissers came up.

She read through the brief descriptions and clicked on the link to an obituary for an Ada Visser who was born in South Bend, Indiana, and died in Cranberry Cove. She read through it quickly. It was brief and didn't offer much information beyond the details of her funeral service and burial. Monica moaned in frustration. If her death had been at all traumatic or suspicious as Janice had suggested, there ought to be an article somewhere.

She finally found a brief entry in the *Cranberry Cove Chronicle* about a Mrs. Ada Visser who had been found dead in her bathtub of a heart attack. Foul play was not suspected. Was it the trauma of having had a heart attack that was causing her to haunt Nancy's cottage?

Monica slapped her forehead. Now she was acting as if the ghost was real and not simply a figment of her mother's imagination. She knew Nancy wasn't going to rest until Monica did everything possible. She might as well get on with it.

She wondered if it was possible to *give* someone a heart attack on purpose? Scare them, maybe?

She typed *causes of a heart attack* into her search engine. Opinion was divided, but it seemed it was possible to scare someone into having a heart attack but the person would already have had to be suffering from advanced heart disease.

There was no way she could access Ada Visser's health records. Or figure out who might have wanted to kill her. Perhaps the best course of action was to find a way to rid Nancy of her ghost—whether that was Ada Visser or someone else. And she knew just the person to ask.

• • •

Monica fed Teddy and then fixed herself some lunch. She finished her turkey sandwich, gave the crusts to Hercule, tidied the kitchen and bundled Teddy into a blue sweater and a knit cap that she tied under his chin. He gleefully pulled on one of the ties and undid the bow Monica had just made. She tied it again and carried him out to the car.

He made gurgling sounds and kicked his feet happily as she drove back into town. The wind had whipped the lake into frothy white-capped waves and a few people walked along the edge, holding their jackets and sweaters closed against the gusts, their faces lifted to the sun.

Monica knew winter was around the corner but right now, she was going to relish the glorious weather.

She pulled into a parking space in front of the Cranberry Cove Diner. The door was cracked open and the scent of hamburgers frying on the griddle and fries sizzling in hot oil drifting out smelled enticing despite the fact she'd already had her lunch. Through the window, she saw Gus at his accustomed spot flipping burgers and eggs with practiced dexterity. Gus was like the mail service, neither snow nor rain nor heat nor gloom of night kept Gus from his position at the diner's grill.

Twilight, Monica's destination, was next to the diner. She wheeled Teddy to the door and opened it. Tempest's crushed velvet tunic rustled as she rushed over and helped Monica maneuver the carriage inside.

Tempest immediately bent down to smile at Teddy and stroke his head. She was delighted when Teddy grabbed her finger and tried to put it in his mouth.

Monica laughed to herself. When she was pregnant, all the attention was lavished on her, but now that Teddy was here, he was the star of the show. Frankly, she was relieved. She'd never been comfortable being the center of attention.

"What a sweetie he is," Tempest said as she straightened up. The amulet hanging from a silk cord around her neck swung back and forth. "Such a good baby. I know just what you need."

Monica was startled. Had Tempest divined the purpose of her visit? Did the crystals give her some sort of superpower?

Tempest bustled behind the counter and began opening various drawers in the tall cabinet that held the crystals she sold. "Here it is!" She placed an opalescent stone on a velvet pad.

"What is it?"

"It's moonstone," Tempest said, handing Monica the stone. "It's for protection, strength and growth. Place it in a corner of the baby's room." She pointed at the crystal in Monica's palm. "See the play of light?" she said, as Monica tilted the moonstone this way and that. "That's called adularescence."

"It's beautiful." Monica wasn't sure she completely believed in the healing properties of crystals, but the stone was lovely. "How much is it?"

Tempest shook her head. "No, no, it's my gift to you and little Teddy."

"Are you sure?"

"Absolutely." Tempest wrapped the stone in pale pink tissue paper and slipped it into a black bag with *Twilight* written in fancy white script on the front.

Monica thanked her and tucked the package into the storage

pouch on Teddy's carriage.

"Seeing Teddy has been a real treat but is there something else I can help you with?"

"Yes, as a matter of fact. My mother thinks her house is haunted." Monica made a face.

"I take it you don't believe in ghosts?"

Monica grimaced. "Not really." She hesitated. "I'm not sure."

"But your mother does, I gather."

Monica nodded. "And it's upsetting her. I said I would see what I could do to help." She bent down and fixed the blanket Teddy had managed to kick off. "Janice thinks the previous owner suffered some sort of trauma that has caused her to come back as a spirit."

"That could be. What do you want to do?"

Monica shrugged. "I thought you might know a way to get rid of it? A crystal perhaps that might banish it or put it to rest?"

Tempest frowned. "There are several things she could do. One of them is to put a ring of salt around the house. A ghost won't cross it."

Monica laughed. "I can't see my mother sprinkling salt around her house. The neighbors might think she'd joined a cult or something."

Tempest tapped her chin with her index finger. "Let me think." She pulled a book from beneath the counter and began to page through it. "There are some crystals that might be helpful. For instance, howlite, tourmaline, and agate."

"Do you have any of those?"

"I recently sold the last of my tourmaline and there isn't much call for howlite, but I should have some agate." She opened another drawer and took out a green stone with bands of various colors running through it. "Agate is good for changing negative energy into positive. It also enhances mental activity and heals inner anxiety and anger. That might be good for your mother's ghost."

Monica laughed. "And good for my mother."

Tempest began to wrap up the stone. "It's perfect then."

As Monica drove back to the farm, she decided she needed a backup plan in case Tempest's crystals didn't work to remove the ghost from her mother's house. Was it possible for a crystal to have a placebo affect? Perhaps her mother would come to her senses and realize that her glasses ended up in her robe pocket because she put them there and something jostled the house and caused the clock to fall off the mantel.

But if not . . .

Chapter 8

As Monica was heading back to the farm, a thought occurred to her. What if her mother's house had been haunted when Ada Visser lived there? It was possible. Perhaps it would reassure her mother to know that the ghost meant no harm. But Ada Visser was dead, so she could hardly ask her. There was a lawyer who handled the sale of the house for the estate, but he would hardly be the one to ask. There had to be family behind the sale who would have inherited the proceeds. Of course, it would be just her luck that Ada Visser had been a spinster who left all her money to an animal sanctuary or some other charity.

There was only one way to find out. Monica pulled over to the side of the road and retrieved her cell phone from her purse. She glanced in her rearview mirror. Teddy was fast asleep, his eyelids fluttering as if he was dreaming.

Monica dialed her mother's number and after a brief conversation, during which Nancy expressed her gratitude to Monica for her pursuit of information, her mother gave her the name and address of the real estate firm she'd dealt with.

Ziegler and Ziegler Realty was on Elm Street several blocks away from the Cranberry Cove library. A rutted driveway led to a parking lot just large enough for three cars. Two spaces were already occupied and Monica pulled into the third.

Teddy hardly stirred as she took him out of his car seat and placed him in a baby sling. She hugged him to her chest as she walked up the cracked cement path leading to the entrance of the building.

Pictures of houses were displayed in the large plate glass window, many of them yellow and curling. It didn't look as if Ziegler and Ziegler was a hotbed of activity.

She was glad she was carrying Teddy and didn't have to maneuver the stroller up the cracked and uneven cement steps leading to the front door. A bell tinkled as she pushed it open.

The small office held three desks. A stocky blond woman was standing at the one in front talking on the telephone. She motioned for Monica to wait and quickly ended the call.

"Welcome." She gestured at the telephone. "I apologize. Our

receptionist is out sick today and Bethany is having her lunch. I'm Sandra Ziegler." Her numerous gold bracelets jangled as she held out her hand. "How can I help you? Buying or selling?"

"Neither, actually." Monica took a seat in front of the desk. Teddy gave a little sigh but mercifully didn't wake up. "This is going to sound ridiculous." Monica suddenly realized just how absurd the whole thing sounded.

Sandra laughed. "You wouldn't believe what we hear in this business." She smoothed the front of her taupe jacquard jacket. "Try me."

Here goes nothing. Monica took a deep breath. "You handled the sale of the house my mother purchased."

Sandra raised her eyebrows. "Does she want to sell?"

"No. Nothing like that. She . . . she thinks the house is haunted. That there's a ghost playing tricks on her."

"That's the first time I've heard that one. Does she want to move?"

"No, not at all. She loves the house but she wants to get rid of the ghost."

Sandra chuckled. "I'm afraid that's a bit beyond my area of expertise. I don't see how I can help you."

"I only want some information about the house."

Sandra pursed her lips. "My daughter Bethany handled that sale, I believe." She turned around and yelled toward the open door. "Bethany. Come out here."

A younger woman appeared in the doorway. Unlike her mother, she was tall and slim to the point of being gaunt. She was wearing a navy-blue suit, had light brown hair scraped back into a ponytail and was holding half a sandwich in one hand and a pair of earbuds in the other.

When she saw Monica, she quickly ducked back into the interior room and reemerged without the sandwich. She brushed some crumbs off her jacket and held out her hand.

"Bethany Gage." She motioned toward the window. "The other Ziegler was my father."

"I have a question about the sale of the property my mother now owns." Monica gave her the address. "I discovered that the house was owned by someone named Ada Visser. What I'm hoping to find out is the name of her next of kin. The sale was handled by a lawyer and none of the relatives was involved."

Bethany was looking confused when her mother cut in.

"I'm afraid we can't give out that information. The next of kin wanted to remain anonymous. I'm sorry."

Monica was disappointed but she suspected that was going to be the case. She thanked them and began to walk toward her car when Sandra came out of the building and got into a late-model BMW.

Monica pretended to fuss with Teddy while Sandra drove out of the parking lot, then she walked back up the path to the entrance of Ziegler and Ziegler. She peered through the window and saw that the main office was empty. Bethany must have gone back to eating her sandwich.

Monica had noticed an old-fashioned Rolodex on the reception desk. If she could sneak a peek at that . . .

Monica eased open the door and winced when the bell tinkled. She paused, trying to think of a reasonable story for her return. She quickly pulled off one of Teddy's socks and stuffed it in her pocket. She could pretend she dropped it in the office and was looking for it if Bethany appeared. Hopefully she'd plugged in her earbuds again and wouldn't hear anything.

She quickly spun the Rolodex wheel until she came to the letter *V* and Ada Visser's card. The address of the house was listed along with information about the lawyer who had handled the estate sale. The lawyer was likely to be as close-lipped as Sandra Ziegler, but she thought it was worth giving it a try.

Teddy whimpered and Monica swayed back and forth praying for him to go back to sleep. She held her breath for a moment but the only sound was his even breathing.

She pulled her phone from her purse and snapped a picture of the card. She was putting her phone away when Bethany appeared in the doorway. She didn't know which of them was more startled.

"Oh," Bethany said.

"Teddy lost his sock," Monica rushed to explain, gesturing at Teddy's bare foot. "I thought he might have kicked it off in here, but I guess not."

She began backing toward the door. "Thanks, for everything." She waved a hand at Bethany.

She didn't take a full breath until she had Teddy tucked into his car seat and she was on her way out of the Ziegler and Ziegler parking lot.

• • •

Monica had invited Gina, Jeff and Lauren over for dinner. She wanted to hear all about their honeymoon, brief though it had been. Jeff needed to get back to the farm, where they were right in the middle of harvesting the cranberries. Despite having an excellent and seasoned crew, Jeff wasn't comfortable being away for too long.

Monica was roasting a chicken that she would glaze with cranberry preserves and honey. Teddy was momentarily content in his baby seat and in the process of discovering his own hands.

She heard the crunch of gravel on the driveway. She wiped her hands on her apron and peeked out the window. Gina was getting out of her Mercedes, holding a bottle of wine in each hand. She used her hip to bump the driver's-side door closed.

Monica had the door open before Gina reached it. "Do you want me to take one of those?" She gestured at the bottles Gina was clasping by the neck.

Gina handed her one and they placed them on the counter.

"I didn't know what you were making so I brought one white and one red." Gina pulled out a kitchen chair and sat down with a grunt.

"I haven't seen Jeff and Lauren since they got back from their honeymoon. I'm anxious to hear all about the trip."

"I'm sure they had a wonderful time, but their real honeymoon will be in February."

"Oh?"

"They're going to Snowmass in Colorado to go skiing. And sit by the fire sipping hot toddies and nibbling on charcuterie. They'll have more time then."

"That's true." Monica began snapping the ends off a pile of green beans. "There's less to do around the farm in winter. Jeff spends most of his time maintaining and repairing the equipment then."

The door opened and a gust of wind blew several leaves across the kitchen floor. Greg greeted Gina and kissed Monica on the cheek.

Monica shivered. "It must be getting colder."

"I wouldn't be surprised if we had a freeze tonight." Greg bent and ruffled Hercule's fur. Mittens had appeared to say hello but was keeping her distance.

Greg had barely finished hanging up his coat when Jeff and Lauren arrived.

They were both glowing, although Monica couldn't tell whether that was from the cold or happiness or possibly both.

"Something smells delicious," Lauren said.

"It does. I hope you've made a lot. I was out at the bogs all day and I'm starved." Jeff took their coats and hung them in the closet.

"I think a five-pound chicken along with green beans almondine, mashed potatoes and a cranberry Bundt cake with vanilla ice cream should be enough to fill you up."

"Stop." Jeff laughed. "You're making me drool. Not to rush you or anything, but how long until dinner?"

"Almost ready."

"Is Teddy sleeping?" Lauren peeked through the oven door.

"He is. But he'll probably be waking up shortly to be fed."

"I can't wait to see him. I imagine he's grown."

Lauren sounded wistful and Monica wondered when she and Jeff were going to start their family. They'd probably want to enjoy being newlyweds for a bit longer first.

The oven timer dinged. Monica donned oven mitts and opened the door. The initial blast of heat made her take a step back before lifting the roasting pan from the rack.

A chorus of ooohs and aaahs greeted the bird, which was roasted to golden perfection and filled the kitchen with its delicious aroma. Monica moved the chicken to a large platter and placed it in the center of the table with a dramatic flourish.

Greg did the honors of carving the bird and the green beans and potatoes were passed around the table. Soon everyone's plate was full and the conversation dwindled to an occasional word here and there as they ate.

Jeff was the first to push his plate away and lean back in his chair with his hands on his stomach. "That was delicious."

Lauren helped clear the table and pass out dessert plates and forks as Monica cut the cranberry Bundt cake and Greg scooped vanilla ice cream on top of each slice.

"Mauricio told me that there was some sort of drama at the

wedding after we left?" Jeff spooned up another piece of cake. "Someone died?"

Monica hesitated. She'd hoped Jolie's murder wouldn't taint the memory of the wedding in Jeff and Lauren's minds.

"Jolie Spencer was found dead in one of the porta-potties." The scene flashed through Monica's mind.

Lauren's hand flew to her mouth. "How dreadful. What happened?"

"It seems she'd been suffocated. The police are investigating the death."

Lauren gasped.

Jeff frowned. "Who is Jolie Spencer?"

"Mick Amentas's plus one. Apparently, they were quietly married without anyone knowing about it."

"Jolie's an unusual name." Lauren dabbed her lips with her napkin. "If I remember my high school French, it means pretty. Oddly enough, I knew a girl whose mother's name was Jolie. Jolie Clawson. Candi Clawson was at our wedding."

"Jolie Clawson remarried. After she was widowed, she married Mick Amentas."

"Seriously?"

Monica nodded. "How do you know Candi?" She knew the expression about it being a small world and all that, but Lauren knowing Mick's new wife and her daughter seemed incredible.

"I'm her son's godmother."

"Candi's?"

"We knew each other when I was in college. We were both working at the Belly Up Bar off campus. I was part-time and Candi was full-time. We had each other's backs while we were working in that place. The bartenders were a bunch of lechers. And the customers." Lauren rolled her eyes.

Jeff was lounging in his seat and Monica noticed him suddenly sit bolt upright, a distressed look on his face and his fists clenched. "If I'd been there, I would have . . ."

"Don't worry. I knew how to handle it." Lauren licked some ice cream off her finger. "I felt sorry for Candi. There's not much of a future waiting tables in a bar. I felt a bit guilty knowing that I was only going to be working there until I graduated college."

"What about the baby?" Greg got up and began to carry the dessert plates to the sink.

"Candi had it rough. She wasn't married and the father went to jail shortly before the baby was born. Candi said he was picking her up after work when the police showed up and arrested him."

"What'd he do?" Jeff reached out and took Lauren's hand.

"Something having to do with drugs, I think." Lauren squeezed Jeff's hand. "And get this, it was Candi's mother, Jolie, who turned her boyfriend in to the police."

"What?" Monica nearly dropped the glass she was holding.

Lauren nodded. "Jolie had her eye on someone else for Candi. Candi was pretty and she had a nice figure. Her mother felt she could do better—marry a doctor or a lawyer or some other professional. She was trying to get Candi together with her podiatrist who'd recently divorced his first wife. She told her to put the baby up for adoption when it came."

Lauren got up from her seat and began to help Monica load the dishwasher.

"Candi was furious, of course. She said her mother had ruined her life and there was no way she was giving up her baby. It was really rough for her. She didn't have a lot of friends so she asked me to be Timothy's godmother."

An alarm sounded and everyone jumped.

"Sorry." Jeff pulled his cell phone from his pocket and glanced at it. "I've got to go." He pushed his chair back and it scraped against the floor. "Mauricio says the temperature is dropping and we're close to having a frost. I've got to be ready to flood the bogs if that happens. The ice will protect the berries."

He kissed Lauren on the cheek. "I shouldn't be too long." He turned to Monica. "Thanks for a delicious dinner, sis." He waved and was out the door.

Later, as Monica was feeding Teddy, she thought about what Lauren had said. Had it been a surprise when Jolie and Candi encountered each other at Jeff and Lauren's wedding? They'd looked to have been arguing when she saw them.

And was it a coincidence that the baby was named Timothy, or had Candi named him after his father?

She thought about Timmy who had delivered the porta-potties.

Was Candi the girl Gina had seen in the truck with him? And was Timothy his son?

No matter what, it sounded as if Candi and her boyfriend both had a strong reason for resenting Jolie. Had they been resentful enough to resort to murder?

Chapter 9

Monica was toasting a piece of cranberry bread when her cell phone rang.

"Hello?"

"Monica, it's Mom. I was wondering if you've found out anything more about the former owner of my house? I really must get rid of this ghost. I can barely sleep at night."

"I told you what Tempest said." Monica tried to loosen her grip on her phone.

"That's all very well and good, but if the neighbors see me outside sprinkling salt around the house, they'll think they're living next door to a witch." She paused. "I hope you can follow up with the lawyer who arranged the estate sale."

Monica rubbed her forehead with her fingers. "I'll see what I can do, okay? I promise."

"Thank you, dear."

Monica hung up the call, groaned, massaged the back of her neck, then plugged a number into her cell phone. With any luck, Lauren would be free to babysit for an hour or two.

• • •

After Monica got Teddy and Lauren settled at her cottage, she turned the radio on in her car as she drove toward the building housing the Perkins, Spitz and Doodeman law firm. According to their website, it was in a strip mall outside of Cranberry Cove and close to the highway.

The weather report came on and the announcer gave the temperature, which was warmer than yesterday's low of thirty-five degrees. That was good, Monica thought. It sounded as if a freeze had been averted and Jeff needn't have worried.

The sun was out and it warmed the car enough for Monica to be able to crack her window open.

The car behind Monica pulled into the other lane and the two cars were briefly side by side. The other car was certainly a lot newer and a lot fancier than Monica's old Ford Focus, which took several tries to start in the morning and had to be coaxed up the hill leading to downtown Cranberry Cove.

The other car began to inch past Monica, the sun's rays bouncing off its sleek black exterior. As it finally passed her, she noticed the Lexus emblem on the back. Where had she recently seen a Lexus? There weren't too many of them around Cranberry Cove except in the summer when tourists flooded the town.

She slammed her hand against the steering wheel when it finally came to her. It had been at Jeff and Lauren's wedding and Heather Spencer had been driving it. It didn't add up. Heather was clearly in financial difficulties—borrowing money from Mickey, trying to get Courtney to help her with her rent. What was she doing with such an expensive car?

Unless. Unless she had been anticipating a windfall when she bought it. Knowing her father was already in hospice, she probably thought it was only a matter of time before she'd inherit her share of the estate. But then along came Jolie Clawson and a monkey wrench was thrown into everyone's plans.

The building housing the offices of Perkins, Spitz and Doodeman had been spruced up with a two-tone paint job of gray and white and a fancy portico shading the front door. Gold lettering spelled out *Perkins, Spitz and Doodeman LLC* across the façade.

Monica opened the door and found herself in a small lobby furnished with several steel-framed black armchairs and a dark gray pin-dot carpet.

She was expecting equally modern décor in the office itself but it was furnished like a stereotypical lawyer's office with a brown leather tufted sofa, wood paneling and a wall of leather-bound law books.

A beautiful but severe-looking blond sat behind the reception desk, her fingers flying over her computer keys.

"Can I help you?"

"I'm Monica Albertson. I'd like to speak to Mr. Spitz if he's free."

"Do you have an appointment?" She clicked a couple of keys on her computer. "I don't see an appointment scheduled." She tapped the monitor with her finger.

She should have called ahead and made an appointment, Monica realized. "Is he busy? It won't take long, I promise."

The receptionist frowned. "What is this in reference to?"

"It's about an estate sale he handled."

"Are you interested in hiring our firm?"

Monica hesitated. "Yes." It came out sounding less forceful than she'd hoped.

The receptionist reached for the telephone. "I'll see if he has a few minutes to talk to you."

While she waited, Monica tried to rehearse what she'd say. It would soon become clear that she'd lied about the purpose of her visit, but perhaps she could get some information from him before he threw her out of his office.

Mr. Spitz wasn't what Monica had expected. Based on the office décor, she'd pictured some crusty old man wearing suspenders and who had wiry gray hair sprouting out of his ears like random weeds in a garden.

Instead, Derek Spitz, as he introduced himself, couldn't have been more than thirty, had thick dark hair and was wearing a suit with a continental cut. Monica was momentarily struck speechless by his appearance.

"So." Derek sat back in his chair and steepled his fingers. "I understand you need Perkins, Spitz and Doodeman to handle an estate sale for you. Did someone refer you to us?"

Monica's mouth was so dry she had to lick her lips before she could speak.

"The Visser family."

"I see." He let his chair back spring upright. "I assume you spoke with Philippa Thomas, the daughter?"

Monica nodded mutely as she made a mental note. Philippa Thomas was obviously the next of kin.

Derek glanced at his watch. "I'd be glad to help you but I'm afraid I have another appointment any minute. Would you mind scheduling something with our receptionist and then we'll have plenty of time to go over the details."

"Absolutely. No problem." Monica gathered up her purse. She couldn't believe her luck. She was getting away scot-free without her ruse being uncovered. She felt almost lightheaded as she walked toward the door.

Derek followed behind and reached out to open the door. Monica had just stepped into the lobby when she heard Derek say, "Philippa.

Lovely to see you. Please come in."

A tall, gawky woman with a crocodile handbag swinging from the crook of her arm rose from one of the chairs and began to walk toward Derek.

She had to be Philippa Thomas, Monica thought. Philippa was an unusual name and what were the odds of Derek having two clients called that.

By the time Monica had exited the lobby, she'd decided what she was going to do.

• • •

Half an hour later, the door to the lobby of Perkins, Spitz and Doodeman opened and Philippa Thomas walked out. Monica had been waiting in her car, nearly dozing in the warmth of the sun. Philippa got into a late-model dark blue Volvo, started it and drove out of the parking lot.

Monica had started the Focus the minute she saw Philippa emerge from the building and she pulled out in back of her. She didn't have any clear idea of what she was going to do. She only knew she wanted to talk to Philippa about Ada Visser and put her mother's concerns about a ghost to rest.

She'd been prepared to corner her in the parking lot of the law firm, but that might have alarmed Philippa. She decided to take a different approach. Hopefully, the woman would be more receptive to her while in her own home.

Monica almost lost sight of the Volvo on the highway but finally caught up in time to take the same exit. She followed the car down tree-lined streets where the houses had sprawling front lawns and three-car garages.

Philippa put on her right blinker and pulled into the driveway of a mid-century modern house with stark lines, an expansive picture window in the front and an off-center entryway.

She watched the garage door go up and the Volvo disappear inside. Moments later, the garage door went down again. She waited another few minutes to give Philippa a chance to hang up her jacket and kick off her shoes—although truth be told, she didn't look like the sort to walk around the house in her stockinged feet.

After she thought enough time had passed, Monica got out of the car and headed up the stone path to the entrance. The front door was painted orange and had three window cutouts in a vertical row. Monica took a deep breath and pushed the starburst-shaped doorbell. Was she about to make a fool of herself? She had to laugh. It certainly wouldn't be the first time.

A shadow momentarily darkened the sidelight and then the door was flung open.

"Can I help you?" Philippa looked around as if she thought Monica might be selling something.

"I have a question about the sale of Ada Visser's house. If you have a minute and wouldn't mind . . ."

Philippa pinched the skin between her eyebrows. "But the sale went through. There weren't any problems. At least the lawyer didn't say anything at the time." She hesitated. "You might as well come in." She held the door open wider.

Monica followed her into a spacious living room where light poured in through the picture window. The furnishings matched the exterior of the house—a sofa covered in an orange and brown geometric pattern, a black leather Eames chair in the corner with a rubber plant in a woven container next to it, and a large abstract painting on the wall.

Philippa invited Monica to sit on the sofa and she took the round, womb-like chair opposite.

"This is rather embarrassing." Monica felt her face flush red. "My mother is the one who purchased your house."

"Actually, the house belonged to my mother. Ada Visser was my mother."

Monica cleared her throat and wet her lips. "My mother seems to think the house is haunted."

"Haunted?" Philippa looked as if someone had just told her the earth was flat.

"My mother thinks she's being visited by a ghost. The ghost of a past owner, someone who suffered a past trauma or who had unfinished business of some sort."

"And you think that might be my mother?"

"I don't know. Possibly. She was the last person to live there."

Philippa blanched, her angular cheekbones looking sharp enough to pierce the skin. "My mother died in the house. It was terribly distressing. She was in the bath. The medical examiner said the death was from natural causes. Mother had had a heart attack and slipped beneath the water."

Philippa's hands were restless, plucking at her skirt and brushing off invisible bits of lint.

"But the medical examiner also said he'd found water in her lungs. That must mean she was alive when she slid into the bath." Philippa looked at her hands, which were clenched in her lap.

"Do you suspect foul play?"

Philippa's mouth twitched. "No. I don't know. The medical examiner insisted there was nothing suspicious about the death, but poor Mother had been so upset right before it happened."

"What was your mother upset about?"

She waved a hand in the air. "Any number of things. The nightmares for one. She kept insisting they were real."

"What kind of nightmares?"

"She claimed a man in a grotesque mask was looking in her window or standing at the foot of her bed. No matter what we said, we couldn't convince her it wasn't real." She twisted her gold wedding band around and around on her finger.

"The doctor said they could be what he called hypnagogic hallucinations." She laughed briefly. "I can't believe I remembered that word."

"It is quite a mouthful." Monica shifted in her seat. "What are these hallucinations?"

"They can be visual like people, animals or geometric shapes, or auditory and physical sensations. In Mother's case, they were mostly visual but occasionally she claimed to have heard someone in her room whispering. The hallucinations occur as you are falling asleep and are in that state between wakefulness and sleep."

"What causes them?"

"Stress for one thing."

"Was your mother particularly stressed?"

"I don't know about stressed but she was terribly upset. Aren't they the same thing, really?"

Philippa jumped to her feet and began to pace in front of the glass and chrome coffee table. "There was a ring that went missing from the drawer in Mother's bedroom. She never took it off. Not until her knuckles became too gnarled with arthritis for it to fit."

She sat down in the chair again and leaned forward, her forearms on her knees. "It had a gold filigree band with a ruby in the center and diamonds on either side. My father gave it to her when they got engaged. Not everyone had a diamond solitaire back then. The ring was a family heirloom.

"We thought she must have misplaced it but we never did find it, even after we'd emptied everything out of the house."

"Do you think it was stolen?"

Philippa shrugged. "It must have been. What else could have happened to it? Things don't disappear into thin air. We had home health aides coming and going all the time. My aunt Alma had been stricken with cancer and came to live with my mother. My mother couldn't take care of her alone. She had a heart condition herself. We needed help. The agency insisted they were trustworthy but you never really know, do you?"

Monica felt her pulse quickening. "Did you by any chance have hospice for your aunt."

"Yes, we did. The doctor recommended it. They were a tremendous help and a real comfort to Aunt Alma."

"Do you happen to remember the name of the hospice?"

Philippa frowned. "Let me see." She went to a small desk in the corner of the room and rifled through the drawer. She pulled out a business card, retrieved a pair of glasses from her pocket and perched them on the end of her nose.

"Here it is." She held up the card. "It was the Loving Hands Hospice."

Chapter 10

Monica was paying attention to the road as she drove away from Philippa Thomas's house, but her mind was elsewhere. Was it possible her mother's ghost was actually the sort of hallucination Philippa had described? Nancy claimed to hear things and smell things and that was consistent with what Philippa had told her. Of course, it didn't explain her glasses appearing in her robe pocket, but Monica was quite certain her mother had placed them there herself even though Nancy continued to vehemently deny it.

Maybe Ada Visser had started to doze off in the bath and it brought on one of those hallucinations? A hallucination frightening enough to give her a heart attack?

Monica continued to think about it as she drove toward Mr. Swifty, a new oil change place that had recently opened. They'd been posting help wanted ads for weeks. She thought she might as well try them since she'd received a twenty percent off coupon in the mail.

Both bays were already occupied and she had to wait in line until they were finished working on the pale green VW minivan ahead of her.

Finally, the van pulled out and the door at Monica's end opened and the technician beckoned her forward. Her palms began to sweat a bit. She was always afraid of ending up in the pit or, worse, running into the poor fellow standing in front of her waving his hand.

She managed to get her car into position without any trouble. While the technician worked, she opened the glove box and rifled through the contents until she found the coupon. She was quite proud of herself—so often the coupons lingered, forgotten in her purse until they were past their expiration date.

The technician came around to her side of the car, wiping his hands on a dirty rag. Monica buzzed down her window.

He held up an item he'd taken from under the hood of her car. Monica felt a sinking feeling. Was something wrong with it?

"You need a new air filter. This one's dirty."

Something clicked in Monica's brain. Greg had warned her they would try to upsell her.

"Thanks." Monica gave him a winning smile. "I'll take the car to my regular mechanic."

The young man grunted, put the air filter back and slammed the hood down. He disappeared inside and reappeared moments later with an invoice. He ripped it off the pad and handed it to Monica.

"You can pay inside." He jerked a thumb over his shoulder.

The door went up, Monica pulled out of the bay and found a place to park.

The wind swirled around the parking lot and whipped grit into her face. Monica brushed it away and looked up at the sky. Dark clouds hovered on the western horizon. She wouldn't be surprised if it began to rain before she got home.

The scent of motor oil crept into the small office attached to the garage and lingered in the air. A clerk with a look of boredom etched onto her features took Monica's invoice and coupon without looking at her.

A young man was standing near the corner having a low-voiced conversation with a woman. He was wearing blue coveralls with *Mr. Swifty* embroidered above the pocket and had a pair of oil-stained gloves tucked under his arm.

The young woman's dangling crystal earrings caught the light as they swung back and forth. Monica was shocked to see it was Candi Clawson.

"How did you lose your job?" Candi's voice rose to a squeak.

"Lou went spastic over the missing porta-potty. He blamed me for it. I tried to talk my way out of it but he wasn't having any of it. Besides, I've got this job now and it pays better. They were practically begging for people to work here." He cupped her chin and rubbed a thumb across her cheek. "Relax, okay? Wait till we get the money from your mother now that she's dead." He took Candi by the shoulders and shook her slightly. "Keep your eye on the prize. Everything we dreamed about. That house on the lake with room for Timothy to play. A trip to Vegas for our honeymoon." He put his hand on the back of Candi's neck. "Even better, we get married in Vegas at one of those wedding chapels where an Elvis impersonator marries us."

Candi's lip trembled. "I feel bad that . . ."

Timmy's expression grew harsh and he cut her off. "Jolie deserved everything she got. Don't forget."

"Shhh. Don't say that." Candi looked around the room. "Someone might hear."

Timmy shrugged a shoulder toward Monica and the clerk at the desk. "What do they care? They don't even know what we're talking about."

Monica, meanwhile, had made slow work of retrieving her wallet from her purse and then extracting her credit card from the slot. She made a great show of examining the invoice as if she expected to find an error.

The clerk cracked her gum impatiently, her hand hovering in the air for Monica's payment.

Monica smiled apologetically and quickly handed over her card.

She'd certainly gotten more out of her oil change than she'd expected. Timmy may believe that his conversation with Candi would be meaningless to anyone but the two of them, but he was wrong. He didn't know it, but what he'd said confirmed that both he and Candi had good reason to want to see Jolie dead.

• • •

Monica felt her stomach growl. Maybe she'd stop at the diner for a bowl of their chili. It wasn't on the menu, and only locals knew about it. Gus claimed it was the best chili in the world, and Monica had to agree with him. She'd never tasted any better.

She pulled into a nearby parking lot, put the car in park and grabbed her cell phone off the passenger seat. Perhaps she'd take Greg something to eat as well and they could have lunch together.

She quickly dialed Lauren's number. Lauren answered the call on the first ring.

"Hello," she whispered.

"Why are you whispering?"

"Teddy's sleeping in his carry cot and I don't want to wake him."

"Don't worry. The pediatrician said to make as much noise as usual so he'll get used to it and be able to sleep through it." Monica switched the phone from her left hand to her right. "Are you two doing okay? Is there any chance you could possibly stay another hour? I don't want to keep you . . ."

"No problem." There was a smile in Lauren's voice. "Don't hurry. Teddy's been a dream and I've gotten a lot done on that grocery store account. I managed to put together a draft of a marketing plan while Teddy was sleeping."

"That's great. I won't be long. Promise."

Monica hung up, tossed the phone back onto the passenger seat and pulled out of the parking lot. She scored an empty space in front of the hardware store and walked down the street to the diner.

The place was bustling with the lunch hour crowd, an egalitarian mix of men in business suits with their ties temporarily loosened and farmers in overalls with mud on their knees.

Monica joined the line that was inching toward the take-out counter. Gus kept things hopping, flipping burgers on the steaming grill and serving up one order after another with lightning speed. Finally, it was Monica's turn and she ordered two bowls of chili. She was about to move to the side to let the next person give their order when Gus turned from the grill and grabbed her arm.

His leathery face with the puckered scar on his cheek from a burn accident was serious.

"You help my nephew Mick, please? The police questioned him in that woman's death. His wife." Gus snorted. "He's innocent. I know it here." He thumped his chest with his fist.

Monica reassured him that she would do what she could. She didn't want to tell him she had no idea who the real killer was.

Moments later, she had two containers of chili in hand and was walking next door to Book 'Em.

"This is a nice surprise," Greg said, leaning over the counter to kiss Monica. "How did you know I was starving?"

"A lucky guess." Monica put their lunch on the counter. Grease, along with the scent of rich spices, was beginning to ooze through the paper bag. "Maybe we can eat in the back." She looked around. "Where is Wilma? She's usually glued to your side."

A customer approached the counter and Monica grabbed the bag and stepped to the side. She was surprised to see the customer was Courtney Spencer.

Courtney had her phone in her hand and put it on the counter as she reached into her Gucci handbag for her wallet. She paused and looked up, her hand still in her purse. "I almost forgot. I meant to ask if the new Pamela Valiant thriller has come in?"

"Yes. Let me get it for you. It's part of the display on the table near the mystery section."

Courtney waved a hand. "No need. I can get it myself." She left her purse and her phone and began to walk toward the back of the store.

A text popped up on her phone and Monica couldn't resist. She put out a finger and spun the phone around. The text was from someone named Lexie.

Did you call the lawyer I told you about? She's a bulldog when it comes to shredding prenups in divorce cases. What that jerk offered you was ridiculous. A pittance. You should never have signed it.

Monica rotated the phone back to its original position just as Courtney reappeared at the counter and placed the book—with *From the Queen of Suspense* splashed across the front in white letters against a blood red background—on the counter.

Monica carried the bag of chili to the stock room to wait for Greg. So, Courtney was getting a divorce. And she'd signed a prenup for what sounded like a paltry sum. She already knew Courtney had expensive tastes. Might she have been furious that her father had married Jolie, thus snatching her inheritance right out from under her nose?

• • •

Monica's mind wandered as she drove back to the farm from Book 'Em, bouncing between Jolie's death, Teddy, the farm and the farm store. The farm store made her think of Mick and a sense of uneasiness settled over her. Was Mick planning to leave? So far, he hadn't said anything, but perhaps he was still waiting for confirmation from that restaurant in Chicago.

And he needed his green card to get that job. Was that the only reason he had married Jolie? And was he hoping to inherit her estate when she died? Would he quit and buy a boat and sail the French Riviera or whatever it was rich people did with their money? Monica pictured Mick lounging on the deck of a luxurious yacht, a steward bringing him a cocktail and a beautiful young woman rubbing suntan lotion on his shoulders. It was a compelling picture, making the money a strong motive for murder. No wonder the police were questioning him.

Not that Monica thought he was guilty. She didn't have anything concrete to back up her feelings, she simply couldn't picture Mick as a killer and the image of him on a yacht faded from her mind.

The more she thought about Mick though, the more uneasy she became. Was he or wasn't he going to leave Sassamanash Farm? It was time to rip off the bandage and ask him outright what his intentions were.

Teddy was awake and gurgling in his carry cot with Hercule standing guard when Monica arrived home.

"I changed him five minutes ago." Lauren gathered her things together. "He was a good boy, weren't you?" She bent over Teddy and tickled him under the chin. "You're lucky to have such an easy baby." She straightened up and looked at Monica. "I hope I'm as lucky."

Was that a hint, Monica wondered, as she walked Lauren to the door, Teddy cradled in her arms? Were Lauren and Jeff expecting? It would be wonderful if they were. Teddy would have a cousin to play with.

After Lauren had gone, she bundled Teddy into a warm sweater, put him in his carriage and maneuvered him out the door. She forgot about Mick as she daydreamed about the possibility of Teddy's having a cousin soon as she pushed the carriage down the path. She pictured a swing set in their new backyard and the two of them playing happily.

The picture didn't last long. Her worries about Mick hit her like a freight train as soon as the farm kitchen came into view.

The dark clouds that had been massing on the horizon had moved in and plump raindrops were beginning to fall. Monica put up the canopy on Teddy's carriage and began to walk faster.

She was so nervous about talking to Mick that she got the stroller stuck on the threshold. Teddy was oblivious to her struggle and continued to coo and blow bubbles. Janice rushed to Monica's aid and they made it inside before the rain intensified.

Mick was at the counter kneading dough studded with bright red cranberries. He smiled when he saw Monica.

Monica parked Teddy next to her mother, who immediately began to fuss over him, and went over to Mick. Her heart was hammering and she wiped her palms on her jeans.

"Can I talk to you for a moment? Privately." Her voice quavered slightly.

Mick drew his eyebrows together. "Sure. Should we go outside?"

Monica shook her head. "It's starting to rain. Let's go into the stockroom."

"What is it?" Mick crossed his arms over his chest.

Monica decided she might as well plunge in. "Are you planning to leave Sassamanash Farm?"

"No! Why would you . . ." Mick hung his head. "You must have heard about the offer from La Nourriture in Chicago."

"Yes. I didn't mean to snoop but I overhead—"

Mick waved for her to stop. "I'm not going. I don't want to leave Cranberry Cove and my uncle Gus. Someday he's going to need someone to take over the diner. He insists he's fine, but being on his feet all day has begun to take its toll."

Monica felt her breath rush out of her. "Oh. That's wonderful."

"How could I leave you?" Mick gave her a quick hug. His expression turned somber. "As long as I don't end up in jail." His mouth turned down at the corners.

"What?"

Mick ran a hand through his hair. "The police have been around again asking questions. Let's face it, the husband is usually the prime suspect." He scrubbed his hands across his face. "Uncle Gus said you'd look into it. Find the real killer." His dark eyes beseeched Monica.

She swallowed hard. "There's not much I can do. It's really up to the police, but if I find out anything, I'll be sure to let Detective Stevens know."

"Thank you." Mick's face relaxed. "Now I'd better get back to work before that dough begins to dry out."

Chapter 11

It was damp and rainy when Monica woke up on Saturday morning. Teddy was demanding to be fed and she slipped into her robe and hurried into the nursery. Satisfied after his feeding, he was content to sit in his bouncy seat while she washed and dressed.

Greg had started breakfast—scrambled eggs, bacon and warm cranberry scones.

"Are you interviewing the nanny today?" Greg slid some eggs onto Monica's plate.

"Yes. She's coming in an hour." Even though it was still relatively far off, Monica felt a pang at the thought of leaving Teddy with someone else. The nanny had been recommended by the Van Velsen sisters and that did make her feel slightly more at ease.

Greg headed off to Book 'Em and Monica straightened up the kitchen. She glanced into the living room to make sure everything was in order. She gave the pillows another plumping and opened the curtains even though there was nothing much to see beyond a rain-streaked window.

Teddy had begun to fuss and she was pacing the floor with him when the front bell rang. Mittens raised her head briefly but Hercule, who had been sound asleep, jumped to his feet and began to bark. He accompanied Monica to the door. She had to tug a bit to get it open. They hardly ever used that entrance and the door had swollen slightly.

A middle-aged woman was standing on the doorstep. She had a blond Dutch boy haircut and glasses with large blue frames.

"Monica? I'm Alice Becker." She smiled at Teddy, who had finally quieted down.

"Won't you come in." Monica motioned for her to have a seat. She was pleased to note that Alice radiated competence and common sense.

Teddy began to fuss again and Alice held out her arms. "Here, let me." She cradled Teddy and cooed to him softly. "He's absolutely adorable." She glanced at Monica. "Your first?"

"Yes."

"What's his name?"

"Theodore but we call him Teddy."

"Congratulations. You have so much joy ahead of you."

Monica leaned back against the chair cushion trying to look relaxed. "Tell me about yourself."

Alice gave her a kindly smile. "I've been a nurse for twenty-five years. My five children are grown and I don't have any grandchildren yet." She held up crossed fingers. "Hoping for some soon."

Five children! She obviously knew her way around caring for a baby.

"What kind of nursing did you do?"

"I started at the Cranberry Cove Hospital in the ER. The work was grueling and when I got pregnant with my first, I transferred to pediatrics. Those patients are a lot more fun. Children are so stoic and most of them barely ever complained." She bounced Teddy up and down slightly. "I eventually ended up doing hospice work, which I did for years, but ultimately I burned out. So much sorrow." She jiggled Teddy. "Babies are much more fun, aren't you, little Teddy."

Monica felt her shoulders relax. It looked like this was going to be okay.

"Although I do miss my colleagues at Loving Hands Hospice. They were a great bunch." She handed Teddy back to Monica.

Monica's ears perked up. Loving Hands Hospice? "Did you know Jolie Clawson, by any chance?"

Alice looked startled. "The woman who was murdered? I didn't know her well. Passing acquaintances, I guess you'd say. Still, what happened to her was terribly sad."

"Did you ever work together?"

She shook her head. "We served in different areas and really only ran into each other at staff meetings or the occasional get-togethers at the office for someone's birthday or retirement." She glanced at Teddy and smiled. "I heard she married well."

"She did. She'd been her husband's nurse, I understand." Monica paused. "Did she get along with the other employees? As far you know," she added.

"There'd been some controversy at work involving another employee. The two of them had been on several jobs together where the client had reported things missing—money, jewelry, and in one case drugs. Jolie suspected her colleague was the culprit and reported him."

"What happened?"

"Her colleague denied it and tried to point the finger at her but ultimately, they believed her. Management couldn't risk a lawsuit from their clients so they let the other employee go."

"Do you know the name of her colleague?"

Alice pursed her lips. "Let me think. I don't remember his first name but his last name was something like timber." She closed her eyes. "It's on the tip of my tongue." She shook her head. "I'm sorry. I just can't remember."

• • •

Could this colleague of Jolie's be another suspect? Monica wondered as she said goodbye to Alice. It would have been easy enough for someone to sneak onto the farm's property. They could have dressed up as one of the catering staff and no one would have been the wiser. Or, they could have gone to the farm earlier and hid somewhere.

But wouldn't they have had to have known that Jolie was going to be at the wedding? As far as Monica could tell, no one knew she'd married Mick so why would anyone expect her to be there?

She didn't have any answers. Hopefully, the police would arrest the killer soon and put everyone's mind at ease.

Monica fed Teddy and then made herself a sandwich while he napped in his carry cot. She glanced at her to-do list. Tuesday was Janice's birthday and she wanted to get her a present. Various ideas went through her mind and she rejected them one by one. Finally, she settled on a nice box of candy from Gumdrops. She knew Janice had a sweet tooth because she often topped off her lunch with a candy bar.

She checked Mittens's and Hercule's food and water bowls and then got Teddy ready to go. He woke up and protested but she knew he would settle down once they were in the car. She wasn't surprised when he was fast asleep again before they were even out of the driveway.

The interview with Alice had gone well. Monica thought she was just the right person to look after Teddy, even if that thought did make her gulp.

Monica passed that same patrol car crouched by the side of the road like a spider waiting to snag its prey. She was on her way down the hill when she noticed in her rearview mirror that someone in a bright red Corvette had been pulled over.

She found a parking spot outside of Bart's Butcher. Bart was in the window arranging a display of roasts and waved when she and Teddy went by.

The sidewalks were more crowded than usual, even for a Saturday, but the crowds would slowly disappear as the last leaves fell from the trees that had lured them to Cranberry Cove in the first place.

The Van Velsens were thrilled to see them. At least they were thrilled to see Teddy, who looked angelic asleep in his carriage.

Hennie turned from the display she was arranging, and Gerda came out from behind the counter, smoothing the skirt of her Black Watch tartan kilt.

Monica had learned to distinguish between them despite their identical looks and outfits. Hennie was the bolder of the two while Gerda tended to let her twin take the lead.

"He looks like you," Gerda said as she bent over the carriage. "All that lovely dark hair."

Hennie frowned. "Nonsense. He's Greg through and through, aren't you, young man?"

Gerda put a hand to her back as she straightened up. "Darned arthritis."

"What can we get for you?" Hennie moved toward a display. "Is it something for you or a present for someone?"

"It's for Janice who works with me at the farm. Her birthday is coming up."

"Maybe a nice gift box of Droste chocolates?" Hennie picked one from the display and held it up.

"Perfect."

"I'll gift wrap it for you," Gerda said, bustling back behind the counter. She reached underneath and pulled out a pair of scissors. "Did you hear the news?" she said as she cut a piece of wrapping paper.

"What news?"

"It was on the local news. WZZZ. I like to watch it while I eat my lunch. Today we had some of the nice erwtensoep I made last night."

Monica had been in Cranberry Cove, where there was a heavy Dutch population, long enough to know that erwtensoep was pea soup.

"I like to make it with sausage but Hennie always says she prefers it with a pork chop. Bart can always be relied on for some good pork."

"What was on the news?" Monica prompted.

"Oh! I almost forgot. It's quite unusual what the police found." She pulled a piece of tape from the dispenser.

"What did they find?"

"A porta-potty. Can you imagine? It had been abandoned in a field down near the DeJonges' farm stand."

For one crazy moment, Monica thought it was the porta-potty the police had taken away from the farm and that it had fallen off the truck.

"That's not all," Hennie said, frowning at Gerda's gift wrapping. "They found something else as well. The remains of some drugs."

"Dope," Gerda said with relish, as if she was proud of knowing the word. Hennie shot her a look. "What? I hear it on *Law and Order* all the time," Gerda shot back with unaccustomed sharpness.

Monica had to smother a smile. Obviously, Gerda thought she was very up-to-date, throwing around words like *dope*.

"What else did they say?" Monica reached into her purse for her wallet.

"There wasn't much else but the reporter did say the porta-potty belonged to a company called Johnny-on-the-Spot."

Was that the missing fourth porta-potty they tried to bill Gina for? Why was it abandoned in a field? And with drugs inside?

Monica's head was spinning as she bid goodbye to Gerda and Hennie and left Gumdrops. What on earth was going on? Why hadn't that fourth porta-potty been delivered to the lot at Johnny-on-the-Spot? Did Timmy abandon it? Did he really want to risk his job by doing that? Or had someone stolen it?

It was all very curious.

• • •

After breakfast on Sunday morning, Monica put Teddy down for a nap. The urge to lie on the sofa with the Sunday paper was strong, but she decided she'd better pack a few more boxes instead. Greg was renting a trailer that afternoon so they could begin taking some of their belongings to their new house. A moving company would be hauling the furniture when they were ready.

She was going to miss her cottage. It was where she and Greg had started their married life and where they had brought Teddy home from the hospital. When she'd moved to Cranberry Cove from Chicago, she'd been depressed over the loss of her café and the death of her fiancé, but in the end, she'd experienced all the joy anyone could ask for. She hoped Jeff and Lauren would appreciate the cottage as much as she had when they moved in.

They'd already finished packing up the bookcase. The living room looked empty without the colorful spines lined up along the shelves. She decided to tackle the linen closet next. Not that there was all that much to pack. Her mother had taught her that you only needed three sets of sheets—one set on the bed, one in the wash and one in the closet.

Hercule stuck his nose in the open cardboard box and snorted several times.

"Do you smell something in there?" She'd picked the carton up from the grocery store's discard pile. She glanced at the label. The contents had been cans of tomatoes. Surely, Hercule didn't find that enticing.

She began pulling sheets and towels off the shelves and packing them in the box. She was labeling the carton when she heard Greg coming up the stairs.

"Hello. I'm back."

Just then Teddy began to fuss in his crib.

"You go feed Teddy, and I'll begin loading the truck," Greg said, hefting the box Monica had packed down the stairs.

Monica changed Teddy and sat in the rocking chair to feed him. By the time she finished, Greg had packed as much as he could in the trailer.

"Ready to go," he called up the stairs.

"I'll be there as soon as I get Teddy ready," Monica said as she tried to maneuver Teddy's arm into the sleeve of his jacket.

She carried him downstairs, grabbed her fleece and headed out to her car. She strapped Teddy into his car seat, started the engine and backed down the driveway.

Greg was already out of sight as she headed toward their new home. Butterflies were rampaging in her stomach, not with nerves but with excitement. The feeling increased as the house came into view, bathed in the afternoon sun. Greg was already parked in the driveway, the door to the trailer was open and half of him had disappeared inside.

Monica put Teddy in his carry cot and walked up the path to the front door. She'd been in the house before, of course, but this time it felt different. She almost had to pinch herself to convince herself it was real.

She opened the front door and stood in the foyer for a moment taking in the scene. The living room was to the left and the hallway led to the combined kitchen and family room, which Monica had had painted a soft sage green. She was pleased with her choice. The room looked warm and inviting with sun pouring in through the large windows.

Greg appeared around the corner with the first load of cartons. They made a thud as he dropped them on the ground. He saw Monica's look and smiled. "Nothing fragile in there, don't worry."

She was about to head to the stairs to check on the upper floor when the front door opened.

"Hello?"

"Mom? I'm in the kitchen."

"Oh, this is lovely," Nancy said, pirouetting as she took in the entire room. She went over to the window and peered out. "It's going to be lovely in the spring when those trees bloom." She put a shopping bag on the counter.

"What's that?" Monica half hoped it was lunch. She was beginning to get hungry.

"It's a smudge kit." She started taking items out of the bag.

"What on earth is a smudge kit? Cleaning supplies?"

Nancy tut-tutted. "Don't be silly. Of course not." She held up a piece of wood. "This is a palo santo stick." She reached into the bag again. "A bundle of white sage." She laid the herbs on the counter. "A feather and an abalone shell."

"What on earth am I going to do with all that? Cast a spell?"

"Not exactly. We're going to cleanse your new house." She held up the piece of wood. "The palo santo stick will bless and heal your space."

"Heal from what?"

"Everything that happened last summer—the murder, the body buried by the trees."

How could she forget? "Okay, what about the rest of those things?" She waved a hand toward the counter.

"The white sage, which we can light with the palo santo"—she held up the stick—"will cleanse the place and drive out any negative energy."

"What about the feather?"

"The feather is to disperse the smoke from the sage." She dug into her handbag and pulled out a lighter. "See? I came prepared." She held up a hand. "But first we have to set an intention."

"Like what?"

"What you want from the smudging. Like bringing light, love, happiness and protection to your home and family."

"Okay." Monica closed her eyes and silently repeated the phrase.

She hoped she was doing this right. Not that she believed in it. But it couldn't hurt.

"Let me put Teddy outside the room. I don't think the smoke would be good for him. I'll still be able to hear him." She glanced at the carry cot. Teddy was fast asleep, both arms over his head.

"Okay."

Nancy clicked the lighter and lit the palo santo stick and handed it to Monica.

"Let the smoke rise." After a minute, she handed Monica the sage stick. "Put this in your right hand and light it so it smolders but there's no flame."

Monica did as she was told. Earthy-smelling smoke rose in the air. "Hold it over the abalone shell to catch any falling ash.

"Now use the feather to spread the smoke."

Monica waved the feather in the air and watched as the smoke swirled around the room. Finally, her mother instructed her to put the smudge stick out in the shell.

"Did Tempest tell you about this—what did you call it?—smudging?"

"No." Nancy began to gather the things together. "It was Janice.

Fortunately, Tempest had some smudge kits in stock. They both recommended it."

Somehow Monica wasn't surprised.

Greg rushed into the room, panic clear on his face. "Do you smell smoke? Is something burning?"

"We were smudging—burning sage to cleanse the house of any negative energy and bring blessings to it and your family." Nancy said it as if it was obvious and she didn't know why Greg was even asking the question.

Greg nodded slowly and looked from Monica to Nancy and back again.

"Okay. If you say so," he said noncommittally.

"With all the things Monica has been involved in—finding that body last summer and solving the murder of that poor elderly woman and now the murder at Jeff and Lauren's wedding—you can use all the good luck you can get."

Greg grimaced. "I can't argue with that."

Chapter 12

"Why don't you two go out to dinner tonight," Nancy said as they headed to their cars.

Monica looked at Greg and raised her eyebrows.

"Go on. It will do you good. Don't make the mistake I did of ignoring your spouse while you care for your new baby. It isn't good for the marriage."

Monica frowned. "But what about Teddy?"

Nancy flapped a hand at her. "Don't be silly. I'll watch little Teddy for you. I can't get enough cuddles with my little grandson." She peered at Teddy in his carriage and carefully tucked the blanket under his chin.

"What do you think?"

Greg put his arm around Monica. "I think it's a splendid idea. I'll get this trailer back to the rental company while you go home and freshen up."

Did she really need freshening up? Monica looked at her sweater and jeans. Both were liberally flecked with dust. Maybe she could use a change of clothes if nothing else.

Teddy was hungry by the time they got home. Monica was in the living room feeding him when the back door opened.

"Yoo-hoo. I'm here," Nancy called out.

Teddy had finished eating and Monica began to burp him.

"Here, let me do that." She held out her arms.

Monica surrendered Teddy and went upstairs to survey her closet. The Pepper Pot wasn't particularly fancy but it wasn't a worn jeans and grubby T-shirt kind of place either. She dug around for her black pants and chose a blouse she'd bought for a friend's bridal shower. She hadn't worn it in ages and prayed it would still fit.

She was brushing her hair when Greg got back from returning the trailer. He whistled when he saw her.

"Don't you look nice." He gave her a kiss. "Let me spruce up a bit and we'll be off."

Greg was ready in no time. He came downstairs smelling of aftershave and with his hair neatly parted and combed. He ushered Monica outside, opened the passenger door and then went around to the driver's side.

"Were you humoring your mother with that thing she was doing? What did you call it?"

"Smudging." Monica hesitated. "I don't know. Intellectually I don't believe in it but deep down there's a part of me that thinks it might do some good. Or at least that part of me hopes it might."

Traffic was light and they made it to the Pepper Pot in good time. They even had the good fortune of finding a parking space nearby.

Monica's stomach growled as soon as they stepped inside. The aroma was intoxicating.

The hostess greeted them, tucked some menus under her arm and led them to a table for two. She put the menus down.

"A server will be with you shortly." Her long black skirt swished as she walked away.

"What are you having?" Greg peered over the top of his menu.

"Everything." Monica laughed. "Maybe the beef stroganoff. Then again, the pasta with sauce Bolognese sounds good too. I'll decide when the server gets here."

"I see Mickey has switched to his fall and winter menu with some heartier dishes." Greg clapped his menu closed. "I'm going for the steak pommes frites. I guess I'm a meat and potatoes kind of guy."

"Have they forgotten us?" Ten minutes had gone by and a server still hadn't appeared. Greg looked around. "Service here is always so prompt."

He was about to get up to see if he could snag the attention of one of the servers when one finally rushed over to their table. His shaggy blond hair had flopped onto his forehead, where beads of sweat were forming.

"I'm sorry for the wait. We're short-staffed tonight."

"No problem." Greg smiled. He motioned for Monica to go ahead.

"I'll have the . . . beef stroganoff, please."

"And the steak pommes frites for me." Greg handed over their menus.

The server scurried away, trying to avoid the customers attempting to get his attention.

Finally, their meal arrived and they began to eat. Monica's fingers itched to get out her cell phone and call her mother to see how she and Teddy were doing.

"Worried about Teddy?"

Monica laughed. "Is it that obvious?"

Greg smiled at her indulgently. "Yes."

They finished their meal and were polishing off a piece of the chocolate cake they'd ordered to share when Mickey came by to say hello. He pulled a chair from an empty table and straddled it. "Sorry about the wait." He ran his hand over the stubble on his chin. "It's been a heck of a night. We're short-staffed."

"So the server said." Monica snared the last bite of the cake.

"Two of my best servers called in sick." Micky rolled his eyes. "Or that's what they told me. I think it's more likely to have been too much partying last night. One of the dishwashers was having a bachelor's party and I heard it got pretty wild."

"Gee, I never had one of those. I guess I missed out." Greg made a sad face and Monica gave him a playful kick under the table.

"I can't picture you having a wild night on the town."

Greg grinned. "I have hidden depths, didn't you know?"

Micky held up a hand in warning. "Don't ask me about my, ahem, past. But I have to say I always took my job seriously whether it was waiting tables or loading trucks. I guess not everyone does. I had someone quit on me, too."

"That's really bad luck." Greg ran a finger over their dessert plate and licked the last bit of chocolate off his finger.

"And with no notice unless you count an hour sufficient notice. Yesterday, she had to leave early to go to some lawyer's office. Something about a will. And then this morning I get a call that she's quitting."

"She must have come into some money." Greg leaned back in his chair.

Mickey's lips tightened. "She'd better pay me back what she owes me then."

Monica got that feeling in the pit of her stomach—like butterflies but not quite—that meant she was going to learn something interesting.

"Is this the server you told us about?" she asked as casually as possible.

"Heather? Yes. I didn't push her because I knew she was in pretty bad financial straits. She'd already been evicted from her apartment and was bunking with Stella, the hostess. In spite of myself, I felt kinda sorry for her."

A server walked over and tapped Mickey on the shoulder.

"Excuse me," he said, swinging the chair back into place at the other table. "Kitchen crisis."

Monica and Greg waved as he walked away.

"That was interesting," Monica said.

Greg cocked his head. "How so?"

"It sounds as if Richard Spencer changed his will at the last minute. Jolie wasn't the beneficiary as his daughters feared, and instead he must have left his money to them after all."

Greg nodded as a server put a plate with the tab on it in front of him. "So, they had no motive to murder Jolie then. That should narrow down the search for the killer considerably."

Monica shook her head. "I'm positive they didn't know they were going to be the ones to inherit the estate. Heather was hitting Courtney up for money and had already borrowed from Mickey. I saw her coming out of the Harborside Bar the other day with this real shady-looking character." Monica made a face. "He had her arm in a tight grip and she looked frightened."

"Do you think he was a loan shark?" The server reappeared and Greg put his credit card on the table.

"Quite possibly." Monica balled up her napkin.

Greg grimaced. "That's serious. Loan sharks don't play around. She must have been desperate for money."

"And Courtney is apparently going through a divorce and it seems as if she signed a prenup that's going to limit how much money she gets. At least it sounded as if it wasn't going to be enough to fuel her expensive lifestyle."

"And in the end, they did get the money." Greg signed the chit the server brought. "It's beginning to look as if Jolie was murdered in vain."

"Unless . . ." Monica's breath caught in her throat. "I overheard Courtney say something like let's just hope Father did what we told him to."

"What do you think she meant by that?"

"I think she told her father to leave the estate to her and Heather. He was ill. On morphine. It's easy to imagine him giving in to her in his weakened state. I get the impression Courtney can be quite forceful when she wants to be."

"And leave nothing to Jolie? She was his wife, after all."

"I don't know." Monica rubbed her forehead. "Maybe it's simply that they thought Jolie murdered their father and they wanted revenge. Who knows if we'll ever know."

• • •

Alice Becker was right on time Monday morning. It was Janice's day off from the farm kitchen, so Monica had arranged for her new nanny to work today. They'd agreed Alice would work on a day-by-day basis until Monica's maternity leave ended and she would be needed full-time.

Stepping into the farm kitchen was like putting on a pair of comfortable old shoes, Monica thought as she opened the door and stepped inside. She took a deep breath, relishing the familiar scents of yeast, sugar and the tang of fresh cranberries.

Mick already had a pan of cranberry biscuits in the oven and Nancy was placing jars of cranberry compote in a cardboard box.

"These are all ready to go. The Cranberry Cove Inn called in an order on Friday." Nancy dropped in the last jar. "Do you think you could deliver them? Mick will help you carry the box to your car."

"No need. I'll use the cart. That will make it easy enough."

Nancy looked doubtful but before she could protest, Monica picked up the box and transferred it to the wheeled cart they used to deliver goods to the farm store.

It was harder to push over the rutted track than Monica expected, but she managed to eventually get to her cottage. She stopped in briefly to check on Teddy but he and Alice seemed to have settled into a happy routine. She felt a pang leaving him, but he was obviously in good hands.

Most of the weekend tourists had gone home and traffic was sparse. Monica pulled into the driveway of the Cranberry Cove Inn. She drove around to the back and pulled up to the loading dock.

One of the prep cooks, his apron still around his waist, came running out pushing a handcart.

"It's getting colder," he said as Monica popped open her trunk. He glanced up at the sky. "Those clouds are blowing in fast." He reached into the trunk, grabbed the carton and placed it on the handcart.

"Thanks," Monica called out as she got in her car and he wheeled the cart away.

The drive back to Sassamanash Farm was uneventful until she came upon a red Kia partially blocking the road. Monica slammed on her brakes and quickly glanced in her rearview mirror, hoping there was no one behind her. There was no guarantee they'd see her and be able to stop in time.

Was the driver ill? Or had they broken down? Monica pulled out her cell phone and dialed the police.

"Cranberry Cove Police Department," a voice answered.

Monica told the officer about the car blocking the road.

"Is there anyone in the car? Do they need medical assistance?"

"I don't think so. I don't see anyone, but let me check."

Someone might have fainted or had a heart attack and had collapsed or slumped below the window.

Monica checked her rearview mirror again and cautiously opened her door. She darted around her car and to the passenger-side window of the other car. At least that way she wouldn't be standing completely in the road.

She peered through the window. There was no one in the car. Strange. Where could they possibly have gone, especially after abandoning their car in such a precarious position?

Monica put her phone to her ear. "No, there isn't anyone in the car," she said to the officer waiting on the line. She glanced through the window again and this time she screamed. The driver's seat was covered in what looked like blood.

• • •

Moments later, two patrol cars came screaming down the street and screeched to a halt several feet from Monica's car. Monica had pulled her car over to the shoulder to get it out of the way.

Four officers jumped out of the cars and one began placing traffic cones across the blocked lane several feet back. One of the older officers used his flashlight to peer through the car window.

A car came down the road and stopped in front of the traffic cones. The driver appeared to be conversing with the officer directing traffic, who immediately removed some of the cones and motioned for the car to go ahead. It pulled up in back of Monica's.

Monica wasn't surprised to see Detective Stevens jump out and come running over.

"Where's the body?" Monica heard her say.

"There isn't one." The officer pushed his hat back and scratched his forehead.

"Set up a search team. Perhaps it's somewhere in that field over there." She pointed behind him.

The officer mumbled something into his radio and motioned for the others to join him. They began to fan out across the field, picking their way through the tall weeds. More patrol cars arrived and the search party grew.

Stevens stood alongside the car, her hands clasped behind her back, and peered through the window. She pulled a handkerchief from her pocket, wrapped it around the door handle, opened the door and stuck her head inside.

She walked over to Monica. "Why did I suspect you were the one who called this in." She grinned. "Trouble does seem to find you."

Monica didn't know what to say.

"So, what happened?"

"Not much, really. I was driving along and suddenly I came to that vehicle partially blocking the road. I didn't see anyone in the driver's seat so I stopped and called your department to send a patrol car to check on it. They asked me to see if anyone was in the car so I did. That's when I noticed the blood." Monica wrapped her arms around herself.

They watched as the men in the field continued searching. They'd already gone quite a distance without finding anything when there was a shout.

Stevens, who had been slouching against Monica's car, jumped to attention. She put her hands on either side of her mouth and yelled, "What is it? Did you find something?"

One of the patrolmen motioned her over. Monica watched as she threaded her way through the knee-high weeds to where the men were standing. Stevens was looking at something on the ground, her hands on her hips. She bent, picked up a stick and began to poke at something.

Not a person then, Monica thought. It must be something else.

Two of the officers stood guard while Stevens and a third one began to walk back toward the road. The officer headed to his patrol car, rooted around in the trunk and reappeared with an evidence bag. He began to make his way back across the field.

Stevens joined Monica again. She was slightly breathless.

"We found a shoe—a high-top sneaker—with what looks like blood on it. The men are going to continue to search." She put a hand on Monica's arm. "You can go home if you like. If I have any more questions, I'll give you a call."

Monica hesitated. Her curiosity was aroused and she was reluctant to leave. She dragged her feet on her way back to her car, and stopped when there was another shout that sounded more urgent this time.

Stevens began to walk across the field, occasionally breaking into a jog. Monica was not about to miss out on whatever had been discovered. She squinted into the distance in an attempt to see what was happening. Stevens was crouched down next to something hidden in the weeds. She pulled her cell phone from her pocket and made a brief call. Finally, she stood up and began to walk back toward the abandoned car.

She was sweating slightly and pulled a tissue from her pocket and wiped her face.

"What is it?" Monica was on pins and needles.

Stevens jerked a shoulder in the direction of the field. "A body."

"A body? So, someone is . . . dead?"

"Sure looks like it."

"Is it the owner of the car?"

"No clue but that does seem likely."

"Did you recognize them?"

"It's a young man, but not someone I know."

Stevens was doling out information like a parent doling out candy to a child. Monica had to stifle the urge to sigh loudly.

"Any idea how he died?"

"That part at least was obvious. I don't need the medical examiner to tell me he was shot in the head." She frowned. "Based on the blood on the driver's seat, it looks as if he was shot while sitting in the car."

"But all of the windows were up and none of them were broken." Monica inhaled sharply. "It must have been his passenger who shot him."

Stevens tapped an index finger against her chin. "Good point. Hopefully whoever did it left some evidence behind." She gave a sharp laugh that was more like a bark. "Like maybe their business card with their name and telephone number." She looked at Monica and said swiftly, "Just kidding. I'm pretty sure it's not going to be that easy." She shaded her eyes with her hands. "Whoever did it must have made off on foot. A team will be searching the area for any clues."

He couldn't have been dragged into the field, Monica thought. There was no sign of flattened weeds indicating the body had been hauled to its current location.

"But the victim managed to get out of the car. He couldn't have died instantly."

"Depends on exactly where the bullet entered, the type of bullet and what sort of damage it did. The ME will be able to tell us more."

A cloud passed overhead, momentarily blocking out the sun and making Monica shiver. She looked out across the field and saw the officers were already encircling the area with crime scene tape. Stevens had gone back to join them. Monica hesitated with her hand on the handle of her car door.

She couldn't stand it. Her curiosity was killing her. She began to wend her way through the weeds toward the scene.

Stevens frowned when she saw her. Monica thought she was about to shoo her away but she managed to get a glimpse of the body.

She gasped and put a hand to her mouth.

"What is it?" Stevens's eyebrows were drawn together. "Do you know who it is?"

Monica gulped. "Yes. I don't know him exactly but I do recognize him."

"And?"

"His name is Timmy. He used to work for Johnny-on-the-Spot. He delivered the porta-potties for Jeff and Lauren's wedding." Monica looked away from the body. "He was fired from his job for losing track of one of the porta-potties, and the last time I saw him he was working at Mr. Swifty's Garage."

As Monica got in her car and prepared to drive away, she noticed the WZZZ van pull up behind her. Apparently, the old adage that news travels fast was true.

She sat for a moment, her hands on the wheel, staring into the distance, where officers were now working the scene. Was there any connection between Timmy's body being found and the missing porta-potty turning up abandoned in a field? The news report said the police found the remains of some drugs in it. Had Timmy been dealing in drugs? Wasn't that what he'd gone to prison for? And did either of those incidents have anything to do with Jolie's death? She had the feeling this whole case was going to turn out to be about money.

Chapter 13

Monica was almost home when her cell phone rang. She pulled onto the shoulder and retrieved her phone.

"It's Gina. You have to join me today at Soul Spring Spa. Kiran has arranged a wonderful new class for us. I've never done it before but it sounds like fun."

"What is it?" Monica hoped Gina couldn't hear the dread in her voice.

"Hula-Hoops! It's the latest thing. It's an amazing workout for the core. It really hits your abdominal muscles and your obliques, leading to a slimmer waist. It also burns fat and calories."

"You're beginning to sound like an infomercial."

"Come on. You've got that babysitter for the day. You might as well take advantage of it."

Monica tried to remember Hula-Hooping as a kid. Had she been any good at it? She couldn't remember but she doubted it. She'd never really gotten the hang of jumping rope either.

But Gina was a force of nature and Monica eventually agreed to go home, change into workout clothes and meet her at the Soul Spring Spa.

Alice was sitting in the living room knitting, keeping a watchful eye on Teddy, who was sleeping in his carry cot, when Monica arrived home. Hercule was doing his part as well, curled up next to the cot and napping with one eye partially open.

"Everything go okay?"

"Just fine. No need to worry. Teddy is a little angel."

Monica let her breath out. "That's good." She hesitated. Would Alice think she was a bad parent if she went out again? "I was thinking of going to an exercise class with my stepmother." It came out as a question instead of a statement.

"Go." Alice made a shooing motion with her hand. "We're perfectly fine. New mothers need some time for themselves or they'll burn out, and that won't do either you or the baby any good."

"Okay. I won't be long."

"Take your time," Alice called out as Monica ran up the stairs.

Monica quickly changed. She looked at herself in the mirror and frowned. If she was going to continue doing this, she'd have to get some proper workout clothes.

Within minutes, she was in the car and on her way to downtown Cranberry Cove. She spotted Gina's Mercedes in the parking lot and was relieved. She realized her palms were sweaty and she dried them on a tissue she dug from her purse. She threw her shoulders back and opened the door to Soul Spring Spa.

The sense of peace the spa created swept over her and her breathing slowed and her fists unclenched. The neutral wall and furniture colors were soothing, the air was lavender-scented and soft music played in the background.

Gina was waiting for her by the cubbies.

"You're going to love this," she said as Monica stashed her purse.

"You've done it before?"

"No, but everything Kiran does is wonderful."

Monica still wasn't persuaded but she followed Gina into the workout room, where a stack of colorful Hula-Hoops waited beside the door.

Kiran was sitting on the floor at the front of the room in Lotus Pose, each ankle crossed over the opposite leg. He urged everyone to take a Hula-Hoop from the stack.

Monica grabbed the one on top but Gina had to wiggle a red one from the middle of the pile.

"It goes with my top," she explained.

Monica began to regret her decision to come even as they began taking their places around the room.

A young woman walked into the room and smiled brightly at everyone as she stood at the front of the class. She had blond hair pulled into a high ponytail, dazzlingly white teeth and a Hula-Hoop hanging from her arm.

It looked as if even Kiran realized how ridiculous Hula-Hooping was at their age and was leaving the instruction to someone else.

Five minutes into the class and Monica was sweating and watching the hands on the clock crawl around the face at a ridiculously slow pace. She lost count of how many times she dropped her Hula-Hoop, but when she looked out of the corner of her eye, she noticed the other participants were having trouble as well.

Ten minutes into the class, she suddenly got the hang of it and began to rather enjoy it. She was sorry when the class ended.

"That was fun, wasn't it?" Gina wiped her face with one of the towels Kiran was handing out.

Monica had to admit it was.

"When is your mother-in-law coming to visit?" She suddenly remembered that the woman's trip had been postponed and Gina had been dreading it.

"She hasn't finalized her plans yet. I wish she would. This waiting is nerve-racking."

"I've noticed you've been the lovely Gina's guest twice now." Kiran came up behind Monica and she jumped. He was as silent as a cat. "Do you think you would like to join the Soul Spring Spa? We have monthly as well as annual plans."

Monica cast around for something to say. "I don't know . . ."

"Come. Let me give you a brochure."

Gina touched Monica's arm. "I'm going to the ladies' room."

Kiran led Monica through a door and into a small office off the workout area.

"Please. Have a seat." He motioned her to a purple chair shaped like an anemone.

His desk was curved and painted turquoise with a black top. The surface was strewn with papers, which rather ruined the voluptuous aesthetic the designer was no doubt going for.

Monica eyed the chair suspiciously. It looked as if it would suddenly clamp closed with her in it.

Kiran pulled out a drawer and rummaged inside. He swore softly under his breath.

"I need to get some more brochures. Please wait here," he said in his breathy voice.

He disappeared through the door and Monica looked around. There was a check sitting on the desk on top of some papers. She glanced at it. It was made out to Alex Timmerman. She'd guessed that Kiran wasn't his real name. She'd looked it up and discovered it meant ray of light in Sanskrit. Had plain old Alex been too boring for him?

But Timmerman? The name reminded her of something or someone. She tried to remember why.

• • •

Kiran's real name teased Monica for the rest of the day. The answer felt as if it was lurking at the edges of her mind and if she could only draw it forward, she would remember what the name reminded her of. She pictured it as a wisp of smoke that, when she went to grab it, dissipated into thin air.

She was focusing on it so intently, the oil heating on the stove for the chicken breasts she was preparing began to sizzle and smoke wafted to the ceiling. Moments later the smoke alarm began to wail.

Greg came rushing into the kitchen, where Monica had opened the window and was fanning the air with a kitchen towel.

"Is everything okay?"

Teddy, who was in his carry cot in the living room, began to yowl.

"Everything's fine." Monica felt her face flush from the exertion of waving the towel. "I'd better see to Teddy."

"I'll get him." Greg turned toward the door. "Good thing we have a new house to go to in case you burn this one down." He gave a cheeky grin and Monica playfully swung the towel in his direction. He ducked and disappeared through the door, chuckling.

Eventually the chicken was cooked without further mishap, although the smell of burning oil lingered in the air as Monica set the plate of chicken Francese on the table.

"You seem distracted tonight." Greg reached for the bowl of green beans. "Is something wrong?"

Monica shook herself out of her reverie. "No. I'm trying to remember something and it's driving me crazy."

"What is it? Maybe I can help?"

Monica sighed. "I don't think so." She cut a piece of chicken and pierced it with her fork. "It's about the name of the fellow that runs that new Soul Spring Spa Gina is so crazy about."

"Wasn't his name something unusual like Kyrie? Sort of an odd fellow, wasn't he?"

"His name is Kiran. But I don't think that's his real name."

"Parents do give their children odd names. Like Apollo and Zephyr. The other day this woman came into the store with a little boy named Ochre." He shrugged. "It makes Theodore sound positively pedestrian."

Monica raised her chin. "I like Theodore. But I don't think that's it. I saw a check on his desk made out to Alex Timmerman. I think that's his real name. And I can't remember what the name reminds me of."

"I had an aunt named Helen Timmerman."

Monica gave him a stern look. "Somehow I don't think that's it."

• • •

They were sitting in the living room after dinner when Greg picked up the remote and switched on the television. After a commercial for stain removal spray ended, the theme song for WZZZ began to play and the news came on.

The camera panned to a weather map with multiple colors swirling across Michigan.

"Heavy rain expected tomorrow," the WZZZ anchor said. "More on that later." He tapped a stack of papers against the desk. "And now over to Liz Jensen, who is at the scene of a suspected murder. What have you got, Liz?"

The camera switched to a young blond woman in a trench coat clutching a microphone. She was standing by the side of the road and several people hovered in the background. Monica thought she recognized Detective Stevens among them.

"I'm at the scene of a grisly murder," Liz said with apparent relish. "This car"—she pointed at Timmy's red Kia—"was found abandoned right here." She pointed at the ground. "The victim was missing. He was found in that field back there." Now she turned slightly and pointed behind her. She faced the camera again. "The victim had been shot in the side of the head." She motioned with her hand. "Here is Detective Stevens, who is handling the case, with further details for you."

Stevens scowled and reluctantly took the proffered microphone. Monica knew she hated these television interviews. She was wearing black pants and a dark blue zippered jacket.

"Yes, the victim was shot in the right side of the head. We'll know more after the medical examiner performs the autopsy. The front seat was covered in blood and we surmise that he crawled out of the car on his own and collapsed in that field behind me. The windows on the car were all up and none were broken so it seems possible the killer was sitting in the car with him. There was no sign of the killer." She paused. "However, we did find something we believe the killer might have left behind. An earring." She held it up. It was in a plastic evidence bag and the camera zoomed in on it. "It's one of those . . ." She made a twirling motion by her ear and looked at Liz desperately.

"Chandelier. It's a chandelier earring."

Stevens gave a brisk nod. "If anyone recognizes the earring, or has any further information, we would appreciate it if you come forward." A telephone number crawled across the bottom of the screen. "We hope to have more details for you soon."

She turned around and quickly walked away.

"And now back to you, Jack." Liz smiled brightly at the camera, as if she was in a beauty pageant and not reporting on a murder scene.

"We have an important public announcement for you," he said in serious tones. "This could save your life." The camera switched to the county sheriff standing behind a desk with a large poster on an easel next to him.

"Thank you, Jack. I'd like to demonstrate an important safety measure that all residents need to be aware of. It might save your life or the life of someone else." He pointed to the poster. "This gesture here is meant to alert a member of law enforcement or the public that you are being held against your will."

He picked up a pointer and tapped it against the poster. "It's quite simple." He put the pointer down. "Simply hold your hand up, palm facing out. Fold your thumb across your palm like this." He held his hand toward the camera. "And then fold your four fingers over your thumb." He straightened his hand and then demonstrated the gesture again. "The more people that know about this, the more successful the initiative will be, so please share this information with your loved ones." He paused, his hand still in the air. "And now back to you, Jack."

"And now for that weather we promised you," Jack said and the weather map flashed on the screen again.

"Looks like we're in for a filthy storm tomorrow." Greg clicked off the television.

Monica barely heard him. She was thinking about that earring that was found in Timmy's car. It reminded her of the ones she noticed Candi wearing at Jeff's wedding. Was it completely innocent or was she the last person to see Timmy alive?

• • •

Monica tossed and turned that night trying to decide what to do. Should she tell Stevens that she had seen Candi in a similar pair of earrings? But maybe it wasn't even hers. Lots of women wore jewelry like that. It would only upset Candi to be questioned by the police so soon after her mother's murder.

She was still thinking about it when she got up the next morning. She was in the kitchen getting ready to feed Teddy when she made up her mind. She picked up her cell phone and dialed Stevens's number.

Stevens was grateful for the tip but, like Monica, she was keeping an open mind as to what the earring meant. Did it belong to Candi and was she a killer? Did it belong to someone else? Or, it was quite possible it had fallen off in Timmy's car at some other point and it was perfectly innocent.

Still, Monica felt a certain relief now that she had told Stevens. She was almost finished feeding Teddy when the telephone rang.

"Hello?"

"Monica, this is Nora."

"Is everything okay? You sound a bit breathless."

"I am actually. Sadie, that's our oldest dachshund, must have eaten something she shouldn't have. She's been sick all morning. I need to take her to the emergency vet."

Monica glanced at Hercule, who was looking at her with his head tilted to one side. She didn't know what she'd do if anything happened to him. He'd appeared at Book 'Em one day, scruffy and skinny, and when his owner couldn't be found, they'd taken him in. He was now such a part of the family, Monica couldn't imagine life without him.

"Do you want me to open the store for you? It's no problem."

"But won't that be too much with the baby and all."

"Teddy will be fine. He's due for a nap and will probably sleep the whole time."

"That's such a relief. I'll get there as soon as I can. Oh, and please say a prayer for Sadie. She means so much to us."

"Well, Teddy, we're going on an outing," she said as she put on his jacket and tied his hat under his chin.

The September air was brisk and while the sky was dark with

clouds, the predicted storm hadn't rolled in yet. Monica was glad she'd grabbed her gloves at the last minute. She glanced into Teddy's carriage to make sure he was covered with his blanket. He had a habit of kicking it off.

She had had to dig through the junk drawer to find the spare key to the store and she put her hand in her pocket to make sure it was still there.

The lock was a bit fiddly but Monica finally got the door open and wheeled Teddy inside. She flicked on the lights and looked around. The residual scent of baked goods lingered in the air.

She parked Teddy behind the counter, removed his jacket and hat and re-covered him with the blanket. He was struggling to keep his eyes open but soon his even breathing told her he was asleep.

Moments later the door opened and Mick wheeled in a cart of freshly baked goods—sugar-encrusted scones and bread studded with bright red cranberries. He unloaded the baskets onto the counter while Monica arranged the pastries in the display case.

Mick sketched a salute and opened the door, the wheels of the cart clattering over the threshold as he trundled it out.

Monica switched the sign hanging in the window from *Closed* to *Open*. She was grateful Teddy was fast asleep because the store suddenly became busy with customers wanting a cup of coffee and something for their breakfast before heading into work. Things were finally beginning to die down when Nora pushed open the door and rushed in.

She was breathing heavily as she hung up her coat and stowed her purse behind the counter. "Was it terribly busy while I was gone?"

"Nothing I couldn't handle. Fortunately, Teddy slept through everything." Monica glanced at the carriage, where Teddy's eyes were still closed.

"That's a blessing." Nora tied on one of the cranberry-themed aprons they'd ordered to sell in the store.

"How is your dog? I hope it wasn't serious."

"The vet doesn't think so but they're keeping Sadie for observation and have her on an IV to get some fluids into her."

"I imagine that's a relief."

"It sure is. That naughty girl will eat anything. One time she stole some frozen chicken breasts off the kitchen counter. Fortunately, she seems to have the digestive system of a goat." Nora laughed. "Has everyone recovered from the wedding? It truly was lovely."

"Just about. Jeff and Lauren are back from their quick honeymoon but looking forward to a longer one this winter."

Nora straightened the display of cranberry compote on the counter. "I've been meaning to tell you . . . it's probably nothing but it's had me a bit worried thinking maybe it was important after all."

"Oh?" Monica's heart sped up slightly. It didn't sound like good news.

"It was when I went to use one of the porta-potties." Nora's face colored slightly. "I noticed this woman sort of lurking around. She was dressed oddly—in jeans and a black pullover. Was she a friend of Jeff or Lauren's, do you suppose? Still, everyone else was dressed in their Sunday best. She didn't look like one of the guests."

Monica stopped with Teddy's jacket in her hand. It could have been anyone, she thought. "Was there anything else unusual about her? Other than how she was dressed?"

"She was blond. Although that's not much help, I know." Nora wrinkled her forehead. "There was one thing. She was very tan. As if she'd been away recently." She laughed. "The rest of us are already working on our usual winter pallor."

Who could it have been? And what was she doing at the wedding? Nora was right. It didn't sound as if she was a guest—certainly not dressed in jeans. Was she part of the catering staff? But wouldn't she have been in the same black pants and white shirt as the others?

And tan. Not many people had a tan this late in the fall. And if she'd been away to some sunny resort, that meant she must have money. At least enough to afford a vacation. Working for a caterer didn't pay all that much.

Teddy began to make gurgling noises as they neared the cottage and managed to kick his blanket off twice before they reached the door.

Hercule gave them a furious greeting and even Mittens wandered over to see what all the commotion was about.

Monica had settled on the sofa and was feeding Teddy when it came to her. She'd seen someone quite recently who had a deep tan. She remembered noticing it at the time. She was putting Teddy down for his nap when she remembered who it was.

The only person she'd seen recently who was blond and tan was Courtney Spencer. What had she been doing lurking around Sassamanash Farm?

• • •

The back door opened and Greg called out, "Hello."

"Goodness." Monica scurried into the kitchen. "Is it that time already?"

"No. I'm early. There's an estate sale I want to go to but I thought I'd grab a bite to eat first." He opened the refrigerator and poked his head inside. "Richard Spencer is supposed to have had an excellent library and he was particularly fond of mysteries and spy novels. There should be some good pickings."

"Richard Spencer?"

Greg turned away from the refrigerator to look at Monica. He raised his eyebrows.

"Jolie, the woman who was killed at Jeff and Lauren's wedding, was married to Richard Spencer before she married Mick." Monica hesitated. "Do you think I could go with you?"

"Want to see how the other half lives, eh?"

Monica got Teddy ready while Greg finished his sandwich. Teddy fussed a bit when Monica buckled him into his car seat but he settled down once they were underway.

Greg plugged the address into the GPS and followed the directions that led them through downtown Cranberry Cove and out into the countryside.

Richard Spencer's spacious Southern Colonial was set amidst other equally large houses with expansive front lawns and manicured gardens. The circular driveway wound around in front of a portico supported by white columns that sheltered a glossy black front door.

Greg whistled. "This is some place, isn't it?" He walked around to the passenger door and helped Monica out. Together they got Teddy settled in his baby sling and walked up the brick path to the entryway.

A discreet sign on the door said *The Spencer Estate Sale. Please Enter.*

Greg turned the shiny brass doorknob and opened the door. They stepped into a spacious foyer with a dark, wide-paneled wood floor covered by a faded Oriental rug. A chandelier hung from the middle of the ceiling.

A woman appeared and approached them, holding out her hand. "You must be Greg Harper. And this must be your lovely wife and baby." She shook Greg's hand. "I'm Betty Doyle, Mr. Spencer's housekeeper. I've been with the family since the girls were little." Her voice was clipped with a slight British accent.

She was wearing a tweed suit that was slightly tight and looked as if she would have been more at home in a pair of casual slacks and sweater. Her steel gray hair was cropped short and her only makeup was a slick of peach lipstick.

She led them down the hall past the spacious living room on the left and a dining room with a fireplace on the right, where discreet white tags were placed on some of the furniture, to the book-lined library. Monica heard Greg's intake of breath as they were ushered into the room.

A man was sitting at the massive mahogany Chippendale-style partner's desk. He was wearing a black suit with a starched white shirt and somber tie. His shiny pate was rimmed with fuzzy white hair and he had a pair of round tortoiseshell glasses perched on the end of his nose.

"Mr. Barrow is from the Barrow Estate Sales and Services and will be glad to help you."

Greg made a beeline for a row of spy novels, their colorful spines a contrast to the more somber dark blues, browns and greens of the leather-bound volumes.

"Would you like a cup of tea?" Betty smiled at Monica.

"That would be lovely."

She led Monica through a butler's pantry with glass-fronted cabinets filled with crystal and china and into a well-equipped but rather dated kitchen. A large window looked out over a velvety green lawn dotted with trees.

"I'll put the kettle on." Betty plugged in an electric teakettle. "I guess we don't put the kettle on so much as turn it on these days." She reached into one of the cabinets and pulled out two utilitarian beige earthenware teacups and saucers. "Do you mind Earl Grey?"

Betty placed a couple of spoonsful of tea in a small china pot. The kettle whistled and she poured the boiling water over the tea leaves.

"We'll let that steep for a minute." She brought the teacups and teapot to the table, pulled out a kitchen chair and sat across from the seat Monica had taken.

"You've been working for the Spencers for a long time," Monica said as Betty poured out the tea. She ran a gentle hand over the top of Teddy's head.

"Over twenty-five years now. The girls have become like daughters to me." She stirred a lump of sugar into her tea. "It was so sad when Mrs. Spencer died. The girls were quite young. I became a sort of surrogate mother to them." She picked up her teacup. "Mr. Spencer tried to be both mother and father to them but he was a busy man."

"He didn't remarry after his wife died?"

"Not until he married that Jolie Clawson while he was on his deathbed." Her lips clamped shut into a thin line. "I was horrified."

"How did the girls feel about it?"

"They were also horrified, of course." Her lips tightened even more. "Especially about the money. They assumed they would be cut out of the will now that their father had remarried. Courtney, in particular, has expensive tastes and whatever she wanted her father bought her." She gave a mirthless laugh. "All except for the pony, of course. She sulked for a week over that.

"I remember Mr. Eastman—he was Mr. Spencer's attorney—was here shortly before Mr. Spencer and that woman were married. I heard him say it was about the will. I assumed Mr. Spencer was arranging to leave his new wife the money."

"Did the girls know what was in their father's will?"

Betty refilled her teacup. "I don't know. I know their father certainly didn't tell them but Mr. Spencer kept a copy of it in his desk. It was still there after he died. I saw Courtney coming out of his office one day and when I went in to dust, I noticed that the top drawer in his desk wasn't closed all the way. I looked to see what the problem was and noticed some papers were keeping it from closing. I checked and saw that it was his will. Someone had been in there snooping. I suspect it was Courtney."

"When was this? Before September twenty-third?"

"Was that a Saturday?" She pinched the skin between her eyebrows. "Usually, I dust Mr. Spencer's office on Wednesdays but that Wednesday I had a dental appointment." She made a face. "I'd broken a crown." She drummed her fingers on the table. "I didn't get around to dusting the office until that Thursday, so yes, it must have been before the twenty-third. My dentist's appointment was on the twentieth."

Monica hesitated. She didn't want to insult Betty. "You didn't happen to get a look at the will, did you?"

Betty drew her head back like a turtle retreating into its shell. "Certainly not. The will was none of my business. If Mr. Spencer had been alive and caught me doing something like that I would have been done for. I would have been shown the door right quick."

"I'm sorry." Monica looked down at her cup of tea. "I didn't mean to sound as if I thought you were snooping. I wondered if you might have gotten a glance at the will when you rearranged the papers so the drawer would close."

"No." Betty's expression was stern. "I didn't find out myself until I was contacted by the lawyer's office. I'm very pleased to say Mr. Spencer left me a generous sum of money for all my years of service. I plan to buy a little cottage in Whitby. It's in Yorkshire on the English coast."

Betty stood up. "I imagine your husband is finished going through the books. I hope he's had some success." Her tone was polite but frosty.

Monica took the hint and pushed back her chair. "Thank you for the tea. That was very kind of you."

"My pleasure." Betty's back was stiff as she led Monica out of the kitchen.

Greg was waiting for them in the hallway, a box loaded with books at his feet.

"All set." He pointed to the carton. "Some wonderful finds. Mary Higgins Clark's *Murder in Manhattan*, and as the French would say, the pièce de résistance, *The Hunt for Red October* by none other than Tom Clancy."

Teddy was beginning to stir as Betty walked them to the door and showed them out.

"You're being awfully quiet," Greg said as they walked toward his station wagon with the carton of books.

"I'm thinking." Monica strapped Teddy in, got into the passenger seat and buckled her seat belt. "According to Betty Doyle, she's almost positive Courtney got a look at the will her father made right before he married Jolie. That was a couple of days before Jeff and Lauren's wedding."

"Did Betty know what was in it?" Greg switched on his blinker.

"No." Monica drummed her fingers on the car's armrest. "But I'm dying to find out."

• • •

Greg pulled into the single parking space next to the back door of Book 'Em. "I hope you don't mind if I run in and leave the books from the estate sale. Or, you can take the car and go home if you want."

"I'll go in with you." Monica opened her door and went around to the rear of the car.

She got Teddy out of his car seat and followed Greg as he dug his keys out of his pocket and unlocked the back door. He switched on the light in the storage room and deposited the box of books on the battered desk he kept for doing paperwork.

"I'll have to do some research on those two first editions," he said as he and Monica went out to the main part of the store.

Several customers were browsing the stacks and smiled at Monica and Teddy as they went by. One older woman with slightly blue-tinted hair went up to Monica and with her face inches from Teddy, made gitchy-gitchy-goo noises at him. Teddy's face began to crumble and Monica apologized and hastily moved away.

Greg went behind the counter, where Wilma was ringing up a customer. Monica put Teddy on her shoulder and he nestled his head into her neck.

"I really wish I knew what was in Richard Spencer's will. It would explain a lot."

Wilma, who had finished with the customer, spun around. "A will? Is the person who made it deceased?"

Monica gave her a puzzled look. "Yes. Why?"

"If the will has been filed with the county, and the beneficiaries have been notified, you should be able to look it up." She pulled her cell phone from her pocket and leaned her elbows on the counter. She tapped several keys and turned the phone around for Monica to see.

"Here you go. County probate court records search." She tapped a few keys. "I'm sending you the link."

"That's wonderful," Monica said. "Thank you."

A customer needing help waved to get their attention and Wilma rushed off to see what was needed.

"Do you think this will is going to tell you what you need to know?"

"I think it's going to make all the difference."

Chapter 14

Teddy began demanding to be fed the minute Monica and Greg pulled into their driveway.

"Okay, okay," Monica said soothingly as she removed him from his car seat and carried him inside. He protested loudly as she quickly changed his diaper. Finally, she sat on the sofa to feed him and his cries dwindled to a whimper and then eventually stopped.

His eyes soon began to close, and when he was finished, Monica carried him upstairs to the nursery and put him in his crib. He stirred briefly but then he quieted down. She tiptoed from the room and went back downstairs.

Her laptop was on the kitchen table and she powered it up. She got distracted by an ad for a new domestic suspense novel that had recently been published but finally closed that window and brought up the site Wilma had texted her.

It took her awhile to work her way through all the instructions but she eventually managed to find what she wanted—Richard Spencer's will.

There was plenty of legalese that forced her to read slowly in order to understand it, but when she was finished, she clearly understood the terms of the will.

The estate was in a trust, but the will made it clear that the bulk of it had been intended for Jolie, save for some bequests to household employees and each of his daughters. However, upon Jolie's death, the remainder of the money would revert back to Heather and Courtney.

Monica blew out a breath and collapsed back in her chair. What she'd uncovered changed everything. If Spencer's daughters knew about this, and Betty Doyle seemed to think they did, it gave them a strong reason to want to be rid of Jolie. Had they resorted to murder to get the money they felt was rightfully theirs?

• • •

Monica had just put Teddy down for his first nap of the day when she heard banging on the back door.

She checked to be sure the baby monitor was on and tiptoed out of the room. "Coming," she called as she rushed down the stairs. She missed the last step and nearly fell but grabbed for the railing and caught herself in time.

She raced into the kitchen, reached for the doorknob to the back door and flung it open. "Gina."

"Goodness, you sound out of breath. You need to do some cardio. They say it's the best way to increase your stamina."

"I was upstairs when you knocked and I ran down the stairs."

"You didn't have to rush."

Monica was about to say something but bit her tongue.

"I have a huge favor to ask you." Gina pulled a piece of paper from her purse and brandished it in front of Monica's face. "That Johnny-on-the-Spot can't seem to get anything right. I should have gone with Porta-Potties Are Us instead but Sylvia, she's one of the women I met at Soul Spring Spa, recommended them."

"What's wrong now?" Monica collapsed into one of the kitchen chairs. She was still breathing heavily from her dash to the door.

"They've charged my credit card not once but twice. Look at that." She put the paper she'd been holding on the table and pointed to two items underlined in red. "Here's my credit card statement. See? Two charges from Johnny-on-the-Spot. Can you believe it?"

Monica stared at the invoice. There were indeed two identical charges. Monica had a sneaking suspicion she knew what the favor Gina mentioned was going to be.

"You want me to straighten this out for you." It was a statement, not a question.

"If you wouldn't mind." Gina batted her eyelashes comically.

Monica sighed. She really didn't want to go back to Johnny-on-the-Spot but it was always so hard to say no to Gina. That must have been how she managed to lure Monica's father away from her mother, although her charms must have worn off because eventually her father left Gina for another woman.

"Will you look into this for me? Please?"

She supposed she could simply phone Johnny-on-the-Spot but she knew she'd probably get further faster in person.

"Okay. I'll go when Teddy wakes up."

"No need to take him along. I'll watch him for you." She handed

Monica the invoice. "What's-her-name is minding the shop for me."

"Is this the same what's-her-name you had a week ago?"

"Yes, it is. Can you believe it? She seems to like me. She even bought a bottle of Thermodynamics from me."

"You're still selling that for Kiran?"

Gina's mouth turned down. "Yes, but I haven't had much luck so far." Her face brightened. "But Kiran is running a sales training session tomorrow and he promises I'll learn some tricks that will send my sales soaring."

Her face fell again. "Mickey's mother has finally booked her flight and she's arriving this afternoon." She held up crossed fingers. "Wish me luck!"

• • •

What had Gina gotten herself into, Monica wondered not for the first time as she drove toward Johnny-on-the-Spot. The whole thing smelled like a scam. What was it called? A pyramid scheme. It sounded as if Kiran was running a pyramid scheme. How many susceptible women had he sucked in besides Gina?

The sun was coming in the car windshield and Monica made a note to wash it as soon as she got home. She flipped the visor down, put on her blinker and drove along the road toward Johnny-on-the-Spot.

She pulled into the parking lot and maneuvered into a space. There was only one other car—a dusty minivan with a baby on board sticker on the rear window.

She locked the car and began to walk toward the door to the office. She was almost there when she noticed a piece of paper with the word *Closed* written on it in black marker taped to the window. Was she going to have to come back? A light was visible in the reception area so perhaps someone was there.

She peered through the glass. Lou's secretary—she thought her name was Steph—had a carton on her desk and was going through the drawers and putting items in the box. Monica noticed the rather sad-looking philodendron peeking out, and the greeting cards that had been lined up along the edge of her desk were gone.

She tried the door and was surprised when it opened.

Steph jumped and made a noise that sounded like a squeal.

"I'm sorry if I scared you." Monica stepped inside.

The dark circles under Steph's eyes looked even larger than the last time Monica had been there. Her weariness was evident in the set of her shoulders and the slowness of her movements. Even her hair was limp and hung listlessly on either side of her face.

"Can I help you?"

Monica pulled Gina's invoice out of her purse and handed it to Steph. "My stepmother was billed twice for the same thing. It's those charges that are underlined in red."

Steph handed the bill back to her. "Not much I can do now, I'm afraid. She'll have to take it up with the credit card company."

Monica looked around. "I saw the sign. Are you closing for good?"

"I'm afraid so. Don, that's my husband, is in a panic. We count on my salary to make ends meet. But I'm sure I'll find something else. Hopefully, something better." She gave a bitter laugh. "The only way to go from here is up."

"Was the business not going well?"

Steph took the worn-looking cardigan off the back of her chair and added it to the box. "It wasn't that. We're closing on account of Lou—he's the owner—being arrested."

"What!"

"The police came in yesterday morning and hauled him off in handcuffs. It's a wonder I didn't burst out laughing."

"What for?"

Steph shrugged. "I don't know exactly but there's certainly been some funny business going on, that's for sure."

"Like what?"

Steph plopped onto her desk chair and scrubbed her hands over her face.

"For starters, the same two people ordered a porta-potty every other week. Who needs a porta-potty that frequently?"

"Were they contractors? They set them up on construction jobs for their workers." Monica remembered seeing one when their house was under construction.

Steph shook her head. "No. Nothing like that. But get this. Lou never billed them for the rentals. And Lou's the type who'd pick a penny up off the sidewalk and think it was his lucky day. No, I do all the invoices, and those two guys were never billed. Not even once."

"Relatives of Lou's maybe?"

"No. Not even friends as far as I can tell. Besides, like I said, what are they using the porta-potties for?" She put her hands palm down on the desk. "It's odd, don't you think?"

• • •

It certainly was odd, Monica thought as she drove home. Even so, there had to be a reason. Why didn't Lou bill those two customers? And what were they doing with the porta-potties?

Monica heard Hercule barking as she pulled into the driveway. It didn't matter whether she'd been gone for hours or only minutes, his greeting was just as enthusiastic.

He was by the door when she opened it, and she bent down so he could lick her face.

Gina came around the corner from the living room with Teddy cradled in her arms. His eyes were wide open and he was attempting to put his fingers in his mouth.

"Looks like you and Teddy got along fine." Monica slipped off her jacket.

"We certainly did, didn't we, snookums." She bounced Teddy up and down. "How did things go at Johnny-on-the-Spot? Are they going to give me a refund?"

"You have to take it up with your credit card company. Johnny-on-the-Spot is permanently closed. I talked to the secretary, who was there packing up her things. She said there was nothing she could do."

"But why?"

"The owner, Lou, was arrested yesterday morning."

"Seriously? Why?"

"She didn't know but she suspected it had something to do with some funny business that had been going on with the company." Monica told Gina what Steph had told her. "I wonder if it has anything to do with that missing fourth porta-potty. The one the police found in that field."

"Maybe something will be on the local news later."

It wasn't until Gina had left and Monica was putting in a load of laundry that something occurred to her. She remembered that the porta-potty abandoned in that field had contained traces of drugs. What if the porta-potties were being used to transfer drugs? Customer number one received a shipment of drugs. He ordered a porta-potty from Lou, placed the drugs inside and the whole thing was subsequently transported back to Lou. Customer number two orders a porta-potty and Lou sends him the one containing the drugs.

Or, maybe Lou received the drugs in the first place and used the porta-potties to transport them to each of his customers.

Had Timmy gotten in the middle somehow and been killed for his troubles?

Hopefully, the police would uncover the truth and WZZZ would report it.

• • •

Teddy was still sleeping so Monica scrolled through some articles on her laptop. On a whim, she plugged Loving Hands Hospice into the search engine. She was startled when an article from the *Cranberry Cove Chronicle* popped up with the headline *Hospice Worker Questioned.* Monica clicked on the link.

The daughter of a Loving Hands Hospice patient, a seemingly healthy middle-aged woman, was found to have died of a heart attack in the middle of the night. "It was completely unexpected," said Warren Barkman, the deceased woman's husband. Barkman also reported that several personal items had gone missing from the home—a coin collection worth several thousand dollars, a small painting by a well-known local artist and a rosary made of amethyst beads. A hospice worker from Loving Hands Hospice was questioned by police but not considered a suspect.

Monica was frustrated. The story contained intriguing details but withheld the name of the hospice worker. Was this related in any way to the death of Ada Visser? Did this woman die a natural death or was there something fishy about it?

A pattern seemed to be forming here, or was it random bad luck? Relatives of two Loving Hands Hospice clients dying mysterious deaths?

Monica read through the article again. The article ended with an interview of a woman named Sheryl Flanagan who was identified as the public relations consultant for Loving Hands Hospice.

Monica was about to power down her laptop when Greg arrived. His face was red from the cold and he was rubbing his hands together to warm them.

"It's gotten quite chilly out there." He put his cheek next to Monica's.

Monica gasped. "That's cold."

"I wouldn't be surprised if we had a frost tonight."

"Poor Jeff. He's going to be worrying about his bogs. It's a good thing the harvest is nearly done." Monica closed the lid on her laptop. "Have you ever heard of a hospice having a public relations consultant?"

Greg scratched the back of his neck. "I don't know. Maybe? It does seem odd that a hospice would need one. A marketing consultant, maybe, but don't public relations firms mostly do damage control?"

"That's what I thought. I'll ask Lauren and see if she knows."

Greg put his hands on the back of Monica's chair. "Want to go out to dinner tonight? I'm sure your mother would be willing to babysit."

"You're probably right. I'm sure she would. She's already complaining she doesn't get to see enough of Teddy." Monica closed her laptop. "I'll ask her."

"How does the Pepper Pot sound? A customer told me Mickey has put cassoulet on the menu and it's delicious. I've been thinking about it all day."

Monica grabbed her cell phone and punched in her mother's number.

"Mom? Mom, what's wrong?" She glanced at Greg. "We'll be there right away."

"What's going on?" Greg reached for the jacket he'd just shed.

"My mother is in some sort of trouble. She didn't say what but asked that we come immediately."

"I'll get Teddy." Greg bolted for the stairs.

Monica put on her own jacket and began to pace the kitchen. Her mother had refused to say what was wrong but she had sounded extremely distressed. There had been other voices in the background as well. A male voice. What was going on?

Teddy already had his jacket on when Greg brought him downstairs. "We're all set."

Monica was grateful they had two car seats so they could leave one in each of their cars. One had been a gift and a friend had loaned them the other one since her toddler had graduated to a booster seat.

The drive to Nancy's house seemed interminable. Monica had to stop herself from biting her nails—something she'd done as a child but had broken herself of in college. There was virtually no one on the road until Greg came up behind a slow-moving tractor pulling a trailer full of hay.

Greg tapped his fingers on the steering wheel, occasionally steering the car to the left in an attempt to see around the tractor, but the road curved ahead, creating a blind spot and there was a double yellow line. Finally, the tractor made a right turn onto a dirt track leading up a hill.

Greg grunted with satisfaction, stepped on the gas and they shot forward.

"I hope this is simply one of my mother's panic attacks over nothing."

"Maybe she saw the ghost again?" The hint of a smile hovered around Greg's mouth.

"Let's hope it's nothing more than that."

Monica had her seat belt unbuckled even before Greg turned into the driveway of Nancy's house. A police cruiser was parked at the curb. The car was empty but its blue and red lights were flashing.

Monica was up the path in a flash, leaving Greg to fetch Teddy from his car seat. She opened the front door and nearly stumbled on the door step, startling her mother, a policeman and another woman she didn't recognize, who were all standing in the living room.

"Monica." Her mother rushed over to her and grabbed her arms. "Thank you for coming."

Greg slipped silently into the room. Teddy was quiet, apparently fascinated by a black-and-white drawing on the wall.

The woman Monica didn't recognize was standing with her arms crossed over her chest and her lips drawn into a thin line. She was wearing an old-fashioned housedress and reminded Monica of Mrs. Gulch from the *Wizard of Oz*.

"There's been a huge misunderstanding," Nancy said in a crisp voice and turned to the policeman.

He cleared his throat. "We had a complaint from Mrs. Albertson's neighbor." He cocked a shoulder in the other woman's direction.

Monica couldn't imagine what on earth her mother had done to warrant a complaint. She obeyed all the rules, never parked in handicap spaces at the store, always returned her shopping cart to the collection area and never ate her French fries with her fingers, even when she was eating at home.

The policeman's leather belt and holster creaked as he moved from one foot to the other. "Mrs. Fernsby here reported suspicious activity at your mother's house."

"What kind of suspicious activity? Was someone trying to break in?" Perhaps Mrs. Fernsby had merely been looking out for Nancy.

"No, nothing like that. It—"

Mrs. Fernsby interrupted. "It was four o'clock in the morning. My acid reflux was bothering me. I got out of bed and went to the kitchen for one of the pills the doctor prescribed for me. I happened to glance out the kitchen window and here's your mother going around her house scattering some white substance on the ground." She glanced at Nancy out of the corner of her eye. "My first thought was that she was practicing some sort of satanic ritual and that made my blood run cold. But then I thought what if she'd lost her mind? She might hurt herself. Or someone else. I couldn't stop thinking about it so I finally rang the police today and asked them to investigate." She glared at the officer. "Took them long enough."

"You could have asked me about it," Nancy protested.

Mrs. Fernsby tightened her arms around herself. "How was I to know what you might do? For all I knew, you might come to the door with a knife in your hand."

Nancy and Monica both opened their mouths but the policeman held up a hand.

"What Mrs. Albertson was doing wasn't against the law."

"Even at four o'clock in the morning!" Mrs. Fernsby objected. "Normal people are asleep in their beds at that time. Or they should be."

Apparently, she didn't see the irony in the fact that she was up at four a.m. looking out her kitchen window, Monica thought.

"What *were* you doing, Mom?"

"I was scattering salt around the house the way Tempest said I should."

This time even the policeman looked startled.

"What on earth were you doing that for? Do you have mice? Although I've never heard of anyone doing that to prevent them. And at four o'clock in the morning."

"I didn't want anyone to see me." Nancy stared rather pointedly at Mrs. Fernsby. "They might think I'd lost my mind." She continued to glare at Mrs. Fernsby.

"May I ask why you were scattering salt around?" the policeman said

"I was told it was a way to get rid of any ghosts in the house."

Mrs. Fernsby threw her hands in the air. "Now I've heard everything."

The policeman leaned back on his heels. "There's nothing illegal about sprinkling salt around your own house. Not even at four in the morning."

Mrs. Fernsby huffed.

He turned to Nancy. "Sorry for any inconvenience, Mrs. Albertson."

Mrs. Fernsby followed him out the door and Monica was disappointed. She wanted to give the woman a piece of her mind.

Teddy began to make discontented noises. "We should go."

"I just hope you're satisfied now that I've tried what you'd suggested," Nancy said in an aggrieved tone.

"I just hope that after all this it actually works," Monica shot back.

Chapter 15

Monica was worried that her mother had been too rattled by her encounter with Mrs. Fernsby and the police to babysit Teddy. "I guess it's back home," she said to Greg as he backed out of the driveway.

"Darn. I could almost taste that cassoulet." He glanced at Monica and smiled.

"Maybe Lauren would babysit?" Monica said doubtfully. "I've already asked her once and I feel bad asking her again. Do you think she'd mind? I don't want her to think we're taking advantage of her."

"Lauren's the sort who is very up-front. If she doesn't want to babysit, I'm sure she wouldn't hesitate to tell you."

"I guess it's worth a try." Monica pulled out her cell and tapped in Lauren's number. After a brief conversation, she hung up.

"Well?"

"She said she'd love to babysit. Jeff is at the Cranberry Cove Yacht Club having drinks with a couple of his buddies and she's all by herself."

"There you go then."

As soon as they got home, Monica changed Teddy's diaper and put him into his pajamas. She was just finishing up when Lauren arrived.

"How is my nephew tonight?" she asked as Monica handed Teddy to her. "He's getting heavier," she said to Monica.

"He was up to twelve pounds at his last doctor's visit."

Monica put on her jacket and was about to leave when she remembered what she'd wanted to ask Lauren.

"You know more about this than I do. Is it normal for a hospice to hire a public relations consultant? Aren't they strictly for damage control?" She explained about the string of complaints received by Loving Hands Hospice.

"PR consultants do other things besides damage control, but in this case, it certainly sounds like that was what they were hired for."

"I thought so." Monica opened the door. "Thanks for watching Teddy. We won't be long."

It was always a wrench leaving Teddy, Monica thought as they drove into town. What was she going to do when it was time to go back to work? She reminded herself that she had faith in Alice Becker, but that didn't completely ease the ache in her heart.

She put it out of her mind as they walked into the Pepper Pot. The aromas alone made her stomach grumble.

The hostess was leading them to their table when Monica spotted Gina sitting at a table in the back with another woman. Could that be Mickey's mother? The woman she was so afraid of meeting and who she was convinced wouldn't approve of her?

She grabbed Greg's arm, apologized to the hostess and led him over to Gina's table.

Gina smiled broadly. "This is Estelle, Mickey's mother."

"Estelle Costello. I remarried after Mickey's father and I divorced. Both of them are dead now."

Monica and Greg introduced themselves.

Estelle appeared to be approximately Monica's mother's age. She was wearing light blue leggings printed with palm trees, a low-cut blue blouse that matched the color of the leggings and a chunky turquoise necklace, matching earrings and a matching cocktail ring. Her nails were painted bright blue and a high-heeled, open-toed shoe dangled from her foot.

It looked as if Gina had met her match.

They each had a martini, straight up, in front of them and were sharing a plate of fried calamari. They appeared to be getting along like a house on fire, as the old saying went.

"What's-her-name is minding the store tomorrow so Estelle and I can go shopping." Gina gestured toward her companion.

"We love the thrill of the hunt, don't we, Gina." Estelle beamed at her companion.

"I guess that's going better than expected," Monica said as she and Greg walked toward their own table.

"Why? Was Gina worried?"

"Worried sick, I'd say. She was afraid Estelle wouldn't approve of her. It looks like Estelle approves of her just fine. As a matter of fact, they look like two peas in a pod."

Greg pulled out Monica's chair and handed her one of the menus the hostess had left on the table.

"I know what I'm having," he said, "how about you?"

"You've talked me into the cassoulet. It sounds yummy."

A waiter appeared at Monica's elbow. "Can I get you something to drink?"

Monica ordered a white wine spritzer while Greg opted for a Scotch and soda.

Monica looked at the waiter. "You look familiar." She snapped her fingers. "You were one of the servers at my brother's wedding."

"I'll never forget it," the waiter said. "It was lovely right up until that lady fell out of the porta-potty."

"I'm sure you'll be dining out on that for weeks," Greg said dryly. The waiter looked confused. Greg shook his head. "Never mind."

"You didn't happen to notice anything unusual that day, did you?"

The waiter frowned. "You a cop or something?"

"No. Nothing like that."

"I did notice the lady that got killed arguing with some guy."

"Did you recognize him?"

"Nah. He was odd-looking though."

"Oh? How?"

The waiter scratched his chin. "I did notice he was bald."

That wasn't much help. At least a quarter of the men at the wedding were in various stages of balding, Monica thought.

"Did you notice anything else? Was he tall? Short?"

"I'd say shortish. He was dressed sort of peculiar too and had a gold earring in one ear and beads around his neck."

Kiran! It had to be. But what did he have to argue with Jolie about?

• • •

It was time for Teddy's two-month pediatrician appointment. Monica gave him a bath and washed his hair—which he didn't like one bit—and dressed him in a new outfit one of her friends from college had just sent.

Greg had already walked Hercule, although Hercule did his best to convince her to take him along on the car ride.

"Sorry, boy, not this time." She scratched his ears. She felt so guilty for saying no that she got a treat out of the cupboard and gave it to him. Since she didn't want to seem as if she was playing favorites, she gave a cat treat to Mittens as well. Mittens wrinkled her nose, sniffed it disdainfully and then finally deigned to eat it.

Teddy quieted down in the car and seemed quite content. Monica had a pang knowing that he wasn't going to be happy about being examined by the doctor. No doubt there would be plenty of tears, especially since he'd be getting his first shots.

The pediatrician was located in an old house that had been converted into offices, just beyond the Golden Scoop and the Soul Spring Spa. There was no parking lot so Monica left the car in a space in front of Danielle's Boutique.

As Monica had suspected, Teddy screamed with rage at the indignity of being weighed and measured, poked with needles and having his ears and eyes checked. He was still red-faced by the time they left the doctor's office, but he'd obviously reached the point where he was too tired to cry anymore.

She was wheeling Teddy down the sidewalk when Gina came out of the Soul Spring Spa, a towel over her shoulder and a sweatband around her head. Her sweatshirt was tied around her waist and her Lycra top was sticking to her back.

Monica hurried to catch up with her. "What was it this time? Hula-Hoops or animal movements?"

"Neither." Gina was slightly breathless. "It was a circus workout." She bent down to look at Teddy in his stroller. "Trapezes and things like that." She touched her shoulder and winced. "I think I pulled a muscle."

"How did things go with Mickey's mother? It looked like you were both having a good time."

"Mickey's mother is a doll! I'm so relieved. I was afraid she was going to be one of those uptight snooty women." She took a deep breath. "I smell something frying. Let's stop in at the diner and get something to eat. I've probably burned a thousand calories in Kiran's class. Come on."

"What about Teddy?"

"What about him? I took Jeff everywhere when he was little. Doesn't that carriage turn into a carrier? I saw someone with one like it the other day."

"But—"

"You can put the carrier on the seat. He'll be fine." She grabbed

Monica's arm and they made their way across the street.

Gus was busy flipping burgers behind the counter but he turned around when Monica and Gina entered. He smiled at Teddy. "Ah, look how big he's gotten."

That was quite the mouthful for Gus, Monica thought. He refused to speak to tourists and he had a hierarchy of greetings he used with residents new to Cranberry Cove, progressing from a slight nod in the beginning to actual spoken words after they'd lived in town for several years.

The lunch crowd hadn't arrived yet and there were plenty of empty booths. The waitress led them to one and slapped some menus on the table. Monica removed Teddy's carrier from the base of the carriage and positioned it on the seat next to her.

When she looked up, she was surprised to see the young man who had been Jeff's best man at the wedding sitting in the booth behind them. She smiled at him uncertainly. He jumped up from his seat.

"Jeff's sister, right? I'm Brian Davis. We were in the Army together and when I say Jeff saved my life, I'm not kidding."

He was powerfully built with broad shoulders and a thick neck. Monica wondered what sort of work he did or whether his physique was perhaps a result of having been in the Army. Jeff had come home the same lanky string bean he'd always been.

"Nice to meet you. I know it meant a lot to Jeff to have you there."

"My pleasure. I wouldn't have missed it. And the chance to meet Jeff's sister. He talked about you a lot when he was overseas. Your letters meant a lot to him."

"Nice to see you again. Enjoy your meal."

Brian returned to his seat and Monica pulled the blanket over Teddy, who had finally fallen asleep, exhausted from his morning at the doctor.

Gina excused herself to use the restroom and Monica scrolled through her phone while she waited.

Brian had a loud, clear voice and she found herself listening to his conversation with his companion.

"You know that woman I've been dating?" Brian said.

"She's married. It's not dating, it's an affair." His friend laughed. "Is this that blond? What's her name?"

"Courtney. Courtney Spencer. Anyway, her husband's divorcing her."

"Lucky for you." He paused. "I guess."

Brian groaned. "Not so lucky at all. She wants me to marry her. She actually crashed my friend Jeff's wedding to tell me . . ." He gulped. "She's pregnant."

"Oh boy, sounds like you're in a bit of trouble. What are you going to do?"

"I don't know. It was a one-off. I didn't mean for things to get serious. I thought she'd stay safely married to that husband of hers."

Gina returned just then and Monica missed the remainder of the conversation. But she'd heard enough. If that had been Courtney at the wedding, she was there to meet Brian, not murder Jolie.

• • •

Monica was already beginning to regret the hamburger and fries she'd ordered as she went back to the car. She had the overwhelming urge to nap. She'd have to feed Teddy when she got home and then perhaps she could lie down for a bit even if the thought did make her feel guilty.

She had almost reached her car when someone grabbed her arm. Monica jumped and spun around.

"You probably don't remember me. I'm a friend of Lauren's and I was at their wedding. I'm Candi Clawson. My mother was the one who was killed."

Monica was so startled she didn't know what to say.

"I need to talk to you." She hustled Monica into the narrow alley between Danielle's Boutique and Twilight. "I hope you can help me."

She was obviously stressed. It showed in the dark circles under her eyes and the tightness around her mouth. Her skin had a dull look to it as if she wasn't getting enough sleep or eating properly, and despite the cool breeze blowing in off the lake, she was wearing a sleeveless T-shirt and a pair of black leggings. Her arms were pimpled with goose bumps.

"You're the one who found Timmy, aren't you?"

Monica glanced at Teddy, who seemed intent on gazing at the metal *No Vehicles Permitted* sign on the brick wall.

Monica hesitated. "I didn't find Timmy exactly. The police did. I only reported that his car had been abandoned by the side of the road."

A single tear rolled down Candi's face. "We were supposed to get married. He promised. But then I found out . . ."

Monica thought she knew what was coming next but she was surprised.

Candi clutched Monica's arm so tightly the skin on her knuckles blanched white. "He fell in with some pretty bad people. Drugs and stuff." She glanced over her shoulder. "His boss at Johnny-on-the-Spot got him involved with it. He thought he could make enough money so we could get married and buy a house."

Candi was quiet as a woman passing by on the sidewalk stared at them.

"Timmy would pick up a porta-potty with the drugs stashed inside and deliver it to some other guy. I don't know if he sold them on the street or they were moved again for someone else to distribute."

Candi looked at the ground. "He didn't know what was going on at first. He thought he was only delivering porta-potties, although it did strike him as odd that these two guys were placing an order something like once a week. My mother always said curiosity killed the cat and she was right. Timmy got curious and one day he took a good look at the porta-potty and found the supply of drugs."

"Did he tell anyone?"

Candi shook her head. "No. Lou paid him real good and he didn't want to lose his job. He sort of looked the other way, kept his head down and went about his business."

"But things changed?" Teddy was getting restless and Monica pushed the carriage back and forth to calm him.

"He figured why should they make all the money while he was risking everything transporting the drugs. If he'd been caught with them, it's not like the police would believe him when he said he had nothing to do with it."

"Why not?"

"He got nicked for selling drugs when he was younger. He did time but got out on parole." She looked over her shoulder again. "But we wanted to get married so he decided to chance it. You know—help himself to some of the drugs. He wasn't going to take a lot so he didn't think anyone would notice."

Monica had to restrain herself from rolling her eyes. "Seriously? Did he really think they wouldn't notice and go after him?"

Candi's face flushed. "Timmy was kinda naïve like that. That's how he ended up in jail in the first place. He trusted people he shouldn't have."

Teddy began to whimper. Monica glanced at her watch. It was almost time for him to be fed. She wondered what it was that Candi wanted from her.

"And now I'm scared." Candi's lip trembled. "I'm afraid they're going to come after me. The guys Timmy got involved with. What if they think I was in on it too?"

"But Lou's been arrested. He can't hurt you now."

"It's not just Lou though. There are others. Lou just works for them." She reached out and grabbed Monica's arm again. "Lauren said you help people. You find the real crooks. Can you help me? I'm scared. I've been getting these calls . . ."

Monica waited but Candi didn't elaborate. "What kind of calls?"

"There's never anyone there. All I hear is someone breathing." She shivered. "It's creepy."

"This is really something you should let the police handle."

Candi looked horrified and Monica thought she was going to run away.

"You don't understand. I can't go to the police. I just can't." Candi let out a sob

Why was Candi so afraid of going to the police? Monica wondered. And was someone really trying to scare her? Maybe she had an overactive imagination. Those calls could be robocalls or kids playing pranks.

Or maybe she had a guilty conscience.

Chapter 16

Teddy's whimper had turned into a wail of epic proportions. Monica didn't want to try to wrestle him into his car seat and then make the nerve-racking drive home. She decided to pop into the Pepper Pot to see if Mickey had a room where she could feed Teddy in peace.

The hostess looked alarmed when Monica pushed open the door and walked in. Teddy's cries, which had reached a crescendo, echoed around the room. He was red in the face and his little hands were balled into fists.

Monica was relieved when Mickey rushed over.

"He's not a very happy little fellow, is he?"

"He's starving. Do you have a quiet spot where I could feed him?"

"No problem." He began walking toward the back of the restaurant and Monica followed him. "The catering manager isn't due in for another hour. You can use her office."

He opened the door to a small but attractive room with two armless upholstered chairs in front of a small desk. Folders were stacked neatly on the surface and a silver-framed photograph was at one end.

"If you need anything, let me know." Mickey closed the door.

Teddy's cries were cut off abruptly as Monica began feeding him. She had wiped his mouth with a cloth and was burping him when the door suddenly opened.

"Oh!"

Monica didn't know who was more surprised, her or the woman standing in the doorway.

She was petite—probably barely reaching five feet tall—with curly red hair and freckles scattered across her nose and cheeks.

"I'm sorry." Monica started to gather her things together.

"No rush. I'm Dee Knolls, the catering manager."

"Monica Albertson. I'm a friend of Mickey's and he said I could use your office to feed Teddy." She motioned to Teddy, who was now fast asleep, the semblance of a smile on his face.

"He's adorable," Dee said as she went behind her desk.

"You catered my brother's wedding. Jeff Albertson. You did a wonderful job."

Dee's face turned slightly pink. Monica wondered how old she was. She looked so young. She had to laugh at herself—she'd obviously reached the age when anyone in their twenties looked young.

"I'm glad it went well. We had some trouble with one of the staff. It's a good thing Mickey has such a good heart." She leaned her elbows on the desk and rested her chin on her hands. "I had to keep an eye on her all the time. She'd often sneak off for a cigarette or to call someone but this time she was toeing the line, at least as far as that's concerned. She did get into a fight with another staff member and I had to separate them. I put Heather on drinks and Owen on the buffet line."

"So, Heather didn't go off at all?"

"Nope. I made sure of it. It's my reputation and the reputation of the Pepper Pot on the line. I didn't want a guest, or worse yet, the host, catching her behind a tree smoking or playing with her phone. How would that look?"

• • •

It wouldn't look good, Monica thought, as she began to prepare dinner. No wonder Dee had been worried about Heather and had kept an eye on her. She couldn't imagine having to deal with an employee like that. She was grateful that Mick, Janice and Kit, who ran Monica's Café in Book 'Em, could all be counted on to do their jobs without supervision.

"What's for dinner?" Greg walked into the living room. He had Teddy in his arms and a burp cloth on his shoulder. "Do you need any help? I can put Teddy in his carry cot."

"No need." Monica lifted the lid on a pot and stirred the spaghetti. "It's a simple dinner tonight, pasta with some of the sauce I made from the summer tomatoes we grew in the garden. I cooked up a big batch and froze some for when I needed it. Now it's paying off." A tendril of hair was curling from the steam rising from the pot, and she brushed it off her forehead.

She turned around, leaned back against the counter and told Greg about her meeting with Dee at the Pepper Pot. "It sounds to me like we can rule Heather out as a suspect. Even though she must have been desperate for money."

Greg shifted Teddy to his other shoulder. "We? You're the sleuth, not me. Although I have to admit to finding this fascinating. Especially since this happened on our watch, so to speak. I think you're right though. It sounds as if Heather wouldn't have had a chance to smoke a cigarette, let alone commit murder."

Monica held out her hands palms up. "But who's left?"

"That's your bailiwick, not mine. I only sell mysteries, I don't solve them." Greg carefully lowered Teddy into his carry cot and hovered over him. He looked up. "Silence. He's well and truly asleep."

"Perfect. Dinner is ready." Monica dished up two plates of spaghetti and put them on the table along with a bowl of salad and a crusty baguette.

Teddy was quiet all through the dinner and only began to stir as Monica filled the dishwasher and Greg washed the pots. She was about to pick him up when her cell phone rang.

"I'll get him." Greg dried his hands on a kitchen towel.

"Hi, Gina," Monica said. "Is everything okay?"

"Fine. But I wanted to tell you about the class Kiran is giving tonight. It's called binaural meditation."

"Does it involve Hula-Hoops or pretending to be an animal?"

Gina was silent for a moment. "No. It has to do with pulsing sounds that help relax you. I thought you might like to join me. You've been looking very uptight lately."

Uptight? Was she uptight? "I really don't think—"

"He's going to turn out the lights and have dozens of candles placed around the room. You don't want to miss this."

She didn't? "I still don't think—"

"I'll pick you up in half an hour. Wear something comfortable."

Before Monica could reply, Gina ended the call.

"Looks like I'm going to a meditation class with Gina. Can you manage Teddy for an hour? I don't think it will be much longer than that."

"Of course. You go have some fun."

We'll see about that, Monica thought as she headed upstairs to find something to wear that Gina would consider comfortable.

• • •

A horn tooted outside while Monica was in the kitchen filling her water bottle. She said goodbye to Greg, kissed Teddy on the forehead and went out the door.

She'd opted to wear a pair of sweatpants and a loose T-shirt. They were the most comfortable things she owned.

Gina was wearing coordinating leggings and a top in a swirling pink and mauve pattern. She glanced at Monica. "You really should up your athleisure wear game."

Athleisure? "Isn't that an oxymoron?"

Gina looked blank.

"It's two contradictory terms put together. Like how can it be athletic wear and leisure wear at the same time?"

Gina stepped on the gas and the car shot forward. Even though she was wearing a seat belt, Monica reflexively grabbed the sides of her seat to steady herself. She held her breath as Gina squeaked through a yellow light that turned red when they were only halfway through the intersection. She was going to need this relaxing meditation class when they finally got to the Soul Spring Spa. Assuming they made it in one piece.

She was about to break into a sweat when they finally arrived at their destination and Gina pulled into a parking spot and turned off the car.

Monica's legs felt wobbly as they walked toward the door. Once inside they were greeted by the sound of soothing music and the ever-present scent of lavender essential oil. Several women were stashing their shoes, phones and purses in the cubbies and a woman with her blond hair in a ponytail was in the corner doing stretches that made Monica hurt just to look at her.

"This way." Gina put her hand on the small of Monica's back to guide her. "It's in the meditation room."

The room was lit by dozens of candles scattered around. Kiran was sitting on a mat at the front of the room, his legs folded into the Lotus position. In his sibilant voice, he instructed them to get comfortable on the mat. He then led them through some simple stretches, such as rolling their shoulders forward and back.

Monica realized Gina had been right. She was uptight. She rolled her head from one side to the other as instructed and some of the tension began to leave her body. They then focused on some breathing exercises that further relaxed her before heading into the binaural meditation. Monica had looked it up and knew it had something to do with different sound frequencies entering the left and right ear.

She was almost disappointed when the class ended and had to admit she felt relaxed as she lay on her mat in Savasana Pose watching the candlelight flickering on the walls.

Suddenly Kiran clapped his hands and turned on the lights. Monica blinked rapidly, startled out of her trance.

The class began to file out of the studio when Gina went up to Kiran to talk to him. Monica wandered around the room, looking at the soothing photographs of waterfalls, sunsets, and clouds in the sky.

"Darling," Kiran called to her and Monica spun around. "Would you be a dear and grab me a towel out of that closet there?" He pointed to a door on the other side of the room.

Monica opened the closet door and looked around. It was too dark to see and she was about to turn on the light when she screamed.

Kiran raced over. "What's wrong? What happened?"

Monica felt a bit embarrassed. "That . . . that thing over there scared me." She pointed to something on the wall. "Is that a mask?" A piece of wood had been carved into the shape of a fierce-looking face with large hooded close-set eyes and an enormous open mouth.

"Oh, that's my Dogon piece. The Dogon are a tribe native to Mali. It's a tribal mask." He chuckled. "I can see how it would scare someone. Especially in the dark."

• • •

So much for her relaxed state. She was now a bundle of nerves. And she still had to face the ride home with Gina. The thought made her want to curl up on her mat in Child's Pose.

The drive home was surprisingly sedate. Obviously, the binaural meditation class had calmed Gina and soothed her nerves.

Greg had already put Teddy down by the time Monica got home. "How was your class?"

"Interesting. It did help me relax but I'm not sure I'd do it again. I guess I prefer a more active form of meditation like walking." She plopped onto the living room sofa. "Kiran has a curious piece of art on the wall in his closet. He said it was a Dogon tribal mask." She shuddered. "It was quite scary-looking. It didn't add to the feeling of relaxation he was going after, which I suppose is why he kept it in the closet and not on the wall in the studio." She brushed a piece of fluff off her sweatpants. "The mask reminded me of something but I can't put my finger on it."

"Sleep on it." Greg yawned. "It may come to you in the morning."

"I hope so." Monica stood up. "I have the strange feeling that it's related to something." She began gathering up the newspaper scattered across the coffee table. "If only I could think of what."

Chapter 17

It was Nancy's birthday and Monica had invited her, Jeff, Lauren, Gina and Estelle for dinner that evening. They were going to have to put a leaf in the kitchen table and it was going to be a bit crowded, but they would manage.

She planned to make Nancy's favorite dish—pork chops baked with apples, mashed potatoes and roasted Brussels sprouts with a balsamic glaze.

She had changed, fed and dressed Teddy while Greg walked Hercule and filled the animals' food and water dishes. Monica grabbed a cranberry scone to eat in the car and within minutes Teddy was buckled in and they were heading to downtown Cranberry Cove and Bart's butcher shop.

"Good morning," Bart sang out when Monica pushed open the door. He rushed out from behind the counter to hold the door while she maneuvered Teddy's carriage into the shop.

Bart retreated back behind the counter and rubbed his hands together. "What can I do you for today?"

"I'm having the family to dinner. It's my mother's birthday. We'll be seven altogether and I thought I'd make pork chops. They're her favorite."

"Ah." Bart cracked his knuckles and perused the display of meat in the case. "Are you baking them or doing them on the stove?"

"I'm making them in the oven with apples."

"You'll want some nice thick ones then. I'd recommend bone-in chops. They're juicier and more flavorful."

Monica smiled. "I trust your judgment."

"Are Jeff and Lauren back from their honeymoon?" Bart reached into the display case and pulled out a tray of chops.

They all looked the same to Monica but Bart looked them over as if they were precious diamonds. She half expected him to pull out a loupe. He finally chose seven that met with his approval and began wrapping them in butcher paper.

He dropped them into a bag. "Here you are." He handed them to Monica as if he was giving her a precious gift.

She put the chops in the carriage basket, paid Bart and wheeled

Teddy outside.

They had to wait a moment for the traffic to clear before dashing across the street to the car.

She glanced at the window of the Soul Spring Spa, where bottles of Kiran's Thermodynamics were arranged in a pyramid, the sun glancing off the capsules inside. A van was parked in the entrance to the spa's parking lot. Dirt clung to the wheels and sides and vague black lettering showed through the white paint.

A man in well-worn jeans slung low on his hips, a T-shirt with *Detroit Lions* across the front and a cigarette dangling from the corner of his mouth was carrying a carton toward the open door of the van. As he got closer, Monica saw that the box was stacked precariously high with bottles of Thermodynamics. Was he one of Kiran's ambassadors? That didn't seem likely. The ambassadors were mostly women like Gina.

He tripped over an uneven patch of macadam and the box tilted slightly. A bottle fell off the top of the stack and rolled toward Monica, finally coming to rest against the wheel of Teddy's carriage. She bent and picked it up and was about to hand it to the fellow when she noticed the bottle was filled with powder and not capsules. Before she could examine it any further, he grabbed it from her and grumbled what sounded like a thank-you.

That was odd. Gina always talked about popping her morning capsule with her breakfast smoothie. Maybe this was a different kind of Thermodynamics? Powder that could be dissolved in a glass of juice or a cup of coffee?

She'd have to ask Gina about it.

• • •

While Teddy napped, Monica looked over the accounting for Sassamanash Farm. She'd taken that job over from Jeff as soon as she'd arrived in Cranberry Cove. He was helpless when it came to numbers, while she had some experience having run her own café in Chicago.

By the time Teddy woke up, Monica had finished with enough time to relax and read a chapter in her book.

"How about going to see Grandma," she said as she changed Teddy's diaper. "We can see if she's had any more ghostly visitors or if the ritual with salt chased them away."

Teddy was a bit squirmy as she tried to put on his jacket but eventually she managed to get it on him and do up the zipper. Maybe she was imagining it, but he seemed excited when she buckled him into his carriage. Obviously even babies probably enjoyed the occasional change of scenery.

Teddy kicked his feet happily as Monica wheeled him down the path toward the farm kitchen. She grasped the knob, opened the door and walked into a scene of pandemonium.

Someone had dropped a bag of flour on the floor and it had burst open. The fan they kept on to cool the kitchen when the ovens were going had sent the flour flying onto every surface and into every crevice. Mick had turned off the fan but the damage had already been done. The place was a mess.

Janice was vigorously wielding a broom, Nancy had a cloth in each hand and was wiping down the surfaces and Mick was trying to rescue the tray of scones he had pulled from the oven right before the catastrophe.

"You need some help," Monica said. "I'll grab the other broom from the storage closet."

"Actually." Nancy put down her cloth for a moment. "I can watch Teddy if you would take a cart of baked goods down to the store."

Mick looked up. "It would be a huge help."

"I'd be glad to. Teddy has had a nap and seems to be in a good mood. And I won't be long." Monica took off Teddy's hat and stowed it in the storage basket. "By the way," she said laughingly as she maneuvered Teddy out of his jacket, "have you had any more ghostly visitors?"

Nancy's lips tightened. "You may think it's funny but I don't." She began to wipe down the table. "That salt thing you told me about seems to have worked. At least so far. Even if I did end up with a visit from the police."

"I am sorry about that, but I'm glad it worked at least."

• • •

Monica trundled the cart loaded with freshly baked cranberry goodies down the worn path to the farm store. She'd walked this way so many times that she felt as if she knew every inch by heart—the tree with the bent trunk that overhung the path, the slight dip where it curved, the protruding tree root.

A couple of cars were in the parking lot when the building came into view. It was showing its age even though Jeff and his crew had painted it over the summer. Jeff had plans to build something new but that was still far in the future.

Two women were sitting together at one of the tables when Monica opened the door. Their heads immediately swiveled toward the cart even though they each had an uneaten pastry in front of them.

Nora came out from behind the counter to help unload the pastries. "Since you're here, do you mind if I nip out for a moment to get some air? I have a headache coming on and fresh air usually helps."

"Of course. Go right ahead." Monica made a shooing motion with her hand.

Nora put on her jacket and quietly slipped out the door as Monica began arranging the baked goods in the display case.

She was placing a paper doily on a platter when the door opened. She was startled to see it was Gerda Van Velsen.

Monica had to blink twice. She couldn't ever remember seeing Gerda without Hennie.

As if she could read Monica's mind, Gerda said, "Hennie's waiting in the car. I never did learn to drive, you see. My first time behind the wheel a deer ran in front of the automobile and I've been too afraid to try again." She glanced in the cabinet.

"Why don't you give me two of the scones," Gerda said, getting a change purse out of her handbag. "We're visiting our friend Grace this afternoon while our niece minds the shop for us. I'm afraid they've had to call in hospice for the poor thing." She lowered her voice and leaned toward Monica. "It's cancer. The same kind that took her mother."

A horn blared outside the shop. "That must be Hennie. She's always so impatient." Gerda shook her head. "Keep your shirt on. I'm coming," she yelled toward the door.

Monica was shocked. Gerda was normally so . . . so . . . she searched for the right word. Mouselike? Timid? She tried to make her voice sound casual. "What hospice is your friend using?"

Gerda put a hand to her heart. "Don't tell me a loved one of yours—"

"Oh, no." Monica waved a hand. "Just curious."

"That's a relief. They've called in Caring Hearts Hospice. Our neighbor used Loving Hands Hospice when her husband's Parkinson's got worse and the doctor said he was nearing the end. She wasn't terribly pleased with them."

"Oh?"

Gerda arched an eyebrow. "After Edward died, she noticed things had gone missing, like a pair of his gold cuff links and her pearl earrings. I had told her not to leave those things out where anyone could see them. She kept them in a little dish on her dressing table. But sadly, she didn't listen." She shook her head. "There were also drugs missing. Narcotics. The poor man was in some pain, I gather." She shook her head. "Not everyone can be trusted. She had a sort of crush on the young man who was her husband's health aide." Gerda tut-tutted. "At her age. Imagine."

"He must have been good-looking. Or charming," Monica said. "Or maybe both."

She placed Gerda's purchase in a white bakery bag, folded down the top and handed it to her. Gerda began to pull out some bills but Monica waved them away. "It's on the house."

"Why thank you, dear." She clutched the bag to her chest. "She did say he was quite charming. No wonder he was charming. He didn't want them to realize he was robbing them blind. Afterward, she learned that the same thing had happened to other clients and they all had had the same home health aide."

"You don't happen to know his name, do you?"

"I certainly do. It was Alex Timmerman."

Chapter 18

Monica was still reeling from what Gerda had told her. Alex Timmerman had worked for Loving Hands, the same hospice Jolie had worked for.

Was Alex Timmerman the person who Jolie reported to Loving Hands Hospice? How could she find out? She thought about it as she wheeled Teddy back to the house but soon pushed it to the back of her mind as she began to prepare for her mother's birthday dinner.

Hercule had appointed himself her helper and dogged her every footstep from the refrigerator, to the counter, to the stove and back again. Monica didn't have to worry about dropping anything on the floor—Hercule vacuumed up any morsels of food as soon as they fell, while Mittens looked on disdainfully at his less-than-gourmet taste.

• • •

The heavenly aroma of baking pork chops and apples greeted the guests as they arrived later that evening.

Gina and Estelle arrived first. "It smells divine in here," Gina said as she shrugged off her jacket. She was dressed for the occasion in purple velvet leggings and a cream-colored satin top with purple sequins adorning the neckline.

Not to be outdone, Estelle was wearing black leather pants, a hot pink top with a sweetheart neckline and sky-high silver stilettos.

"I wish my Micky could be here." Estelle handed her jacket to Monica.

Gina sighed. "Such is the life of a restaurateur, unfortunately."

"You've made my favorite." Nancy clapped her hands together as she sniffed the air upon her arrival. "Thank you, darling."

The door opened and a welcome burst of chilly air swept across the warm kitchen.

"I'm starving," Lauren said, brushing a strand of hair off her forehead. "Jeff just finished up for the day and is taking a quick shower. He'll be along shortly."

Greg arrived right on Lauren's heels. "Hope I'm not late." He closed his eyes and sniffed the air. "Whatever you're cooking, it smells delicious." He patted Hercule on the head. "I'll take Hercule out while I still have my coat on." He whistled. "Here, Hercule."

Hercule was loathe to leave his prime spot by the stove but eventually gave in, and Greg got his leash on him.

Monica opened the oven to peek at the chops and the fragrant steam filled the kitchen.

"I wish Greg would hurry up." Gina sat down at the table. "I'm starved."

"Don't worry. I doubt Hercule wants to be away from the kitchen for very long."

She'd barely finished the sentence when the back door opened and Hercule yanked Greg into the room. As soon as his leash was removed, he raced back to his spot by the stove.

The door opened and Jeff walked in. "Hello, everyone." He hung up his jacket and pulled out a chair.

Monica removed the pan from the oven and transferred the pork chops and baked apples to a platter. Greg took it from her and placed it in the center of the table while Monica dressed the salad.

Finally, everyone had been served and Monica was able to sit down.

"By the way," Gina said as she reached for the salt shaker. "Estelle has decided to become an ambassador of Soul Spring Spa. She'll be selling Thermodynamics with me." She glanced at Estelle and smiled.

"How is that going, by the way?" Greg speared a piece of his pork chop.

"It's going great." A flush crept up Gina's neck that made Monica suspect things were far from great. "And now that I've taken Estelle under my wing, things should really take off. She's a great saleswoman."

Estelle pretended to look embarrassed. "I don't know about that, but I did win the salesperson of the year award when I worked at Neiman Marcus."

"That reminds me." Monica put down her fork. "Thermodynamics comes in capsules, doesn't it?"

Gina reached for her wineglass. "Yes. Why?"

Monica explained about the man picking up a carton from the Soul Spring Spa. "He dropped a bottle and it rolled over toward where I was standing. I picked it up to hand it back to him and I noticed the bottle contained a powder, not capsules."

Gina cocked her head. "That's odd. The ones I'm taking are capsules."

"Maybe it's new?"

Gina scowled. "You'd think Kiran would have told his ambassadors about it. I had someone say she didn't like to swallow pills. If you could simply stir the powder into your morning glass of orange juice, customers might prefer it. I'll have to ask Kiran about it next time I see him."

As she lit the candles on her mother's cake, Monica wondered why that man had been taking cartons of Thermodynamics out to his van. She thought at the time that he didn't look like the type to become a Soul Spring Spa Ambassador. The idea was laughable.

And if Thermodynamics in powder form was a new product, you would think he'd be delivering them to the spa, not taking them away. And surely Kiran would be anxious to get the product into the hands of his salespeople.

It was a mystery but certainly a minor one. She needed to concentrate on figuring out who killed Jolie and Timmy.

• • •

Monica woke in a panic the next morning. At first, she couldn't imagine why. The bedcovers were twisted into a coil as if she had been clutching at them during the night and her nightgown was damp with perspiration.

"Are you okay?" Greg leaned over her, smoothing her hair back from her forehead. "It sounded as if you were trying to fight something off in your sleep."

Monica blinked and leaned against the pillows, which were bunched up behind her. They looked as if she'd been pummeling them in her sleep.

Finally, it dawned on her. A nightmare had woken her. It was returning in bits and pieces—a scary face looming over her, its eyes wide open and wild. Her breathing began to return to normal and her heart slowed to its regular rhythm. Sun was streaming through the window and the dream was rapidly dissipating into the morning air.

"It was a nightmare." She turned to Greg. His mere presence was reassuring. "Just a bad dream."

The creature in her dream had reminded her of something she'd seen before. Monica thought about it as she took a shower and brushed her teeth. Had there been something like it in a movie? Or on television? She was hardly the one to watch horror shows. She was feeding Teddy when it came to her. The face in her dream had resembled Kiran's African mask. That must have been what had caused her nightmare.

She was relieved to have figured out what had probably caused her nightmare but the sense of fear that had gripped her in her sleep still lingered and she couldn't put it out of her mind. She was missing something but every time the answer was within reach, it floated beyond her grasp.

Finally, it came to her. She powered up her laptop and went to her favorite search engine. In minutes, she had found what she wanted and a document was cranking out of the printer. She gathered the papers together and glanced at the clock. She was going to pay someone a visit. Hopefully Philippa Thomas would be at home.

• • •

The neighborhood was quiet, a lawn mower droning in the distance the only sound as Monica drove down the street toward Philippa's house. She glanced in her rearview mirror. Teddy was happily trying to stuff his fist in his mouth. She hoped he would continue to be content long enough for her to talk to Philippa.

She pulled into Philippa's driveway and turned off her car, although she didn't immediately get out. Was this a wild-goose chase? Perhaps Philippa wouldn't even agree to talk to her. The image of a door slamming in her face nearly had her fleeing back to Sassamanash Farm.

She closed her eyes, counted to ten, and got out of the car. Teddy's eyelids were drooping as she tucked him into his sling and they walked up the path to the front door.

Monica rang the doorbell. Her heartbeat sped up and her mouth was dry. She wasn't normally so nervous—it must be the postpartum hormones wreaking havoc on her.

The door was answered quickly and Philippa stood staring at her quizzically. She had an apron tied around her waist and was holding a spatula in one hand.

There was a moment of awkward silence when Philippa said, "It's Monica, isn't it?"

Monica nodded. "I'm sorry. I'm interrupting." She half turned to leave.

"Not at all. Please come in." Philippa opened the door wider. "I hope you don't mind. I'm making a batch of cookies for a friend who's hosting a bridal shower for her daughter." She led Monica into a kitchen, where a mixing bowl sat on the counter alongside a cookie sheet.

The cabinets and countertops were pink and the oven was set into a brick wall with a canvas spattered with red, black and orange paint hanging next to it.

Monica wasn't sure how to begin but Philippa spoke first. "Do you have more questions about the sale of my mother's house?" She scooped up dough from the bowl with a spoon and placed it on the cookie sheet.

"Not exactly." Monica rummaged in her handbag and pulled out a sheet of folded paper.

She'd managed to find photographs of masks similar to the one in Kiran's closet.

"Do you think these images look like the ones in the nightmares your mother described to you?"

Philippa studied the paper, which suddenly began to shake in her hand.

"I must show you something." She held up a finger. "I'll only be a minute," she said and left the room.

Monica was beginning to feel more at ease. At least Philippa hadn't immediately thrown her out. Teddy moved restlessly in his sleep and Monica prayed he wouldn't wake up. She rocked from side to side and he settled down again.

Philippa was holding several pieces of paper when she came back into the room.

"My mother was something of an artist. She used to paint before her arthritis made her hands so painful and deformed. She was quite good. She had exhibitions in Chicago and Detroit." She put the papers down on the counter and motioned for Monica to take a look.

Monica had to stifle a gasp. The pictures looked almost exactly like Kiran's African mask.

Philippa pointed at them. "She had trouble holding the pencil and had to rest frequently, but she said this is what her hallucinations looked like." She took a deep breath. "Only she thought they were real and not something she'd dreamt. The poor thing was almost too scared to go to sleep. She dreaded these visions." She looked at Monica. "But how did you know? How did you know what they looked like?"

"I don't think your mother was hallucinating," Monica said as gently as possible. "And she wasn't dreaming either. What she saw was real. You said you had Loving Hands Hospice for your aunt?"

Philippa nodded. "But I don't see what—"

Monica held up a hand. "Was one of the home health aides that visited named Alex Timmerman?"

Philippa frowned. "It was quite a while ago. Let me think." She drummed her fingers on the counter. "I think there was an Alex. I don't know about his last name though. I'm not sure I ever knew it."

"A man named Alex Timmerman owns the Soul Spring Spa in Cranberry Cove. He goes by the name Kiran now. He owns an African mask that looks exactly like that." She pointed at the picture drawn by Philippa's mother.

"Where are you going with this? Do you think he showed my mother a photo of this African mask he owns and that scared her and led to her hallucinations?"

Monica shook her head. "No. I think he showed her the mask itself. Although he didn't show it to her—he scared her with it. He waited until she was nearly falling asleep and then terrorized her. I imagine he insisted that her nightmares weren't real."

"Now that you mention it, I do remember him reassuring her after one of her bad dreams." Philippa stopped pacing and leaned against the counter. "But why? Why would he do something like that?"

"It's only a guess but it makes sense. I think your mother knew he took her engagement ring and she threatened to go to the authorities. At the very least she planned to tell his employer. Did your mother take medication for her heart condition?"

"Yes. Several pills a day."

"So, it would have been easy for Alex to deduce her heart was fragile."

"I suppose so."

"They say you can cause a heart attack by scaring a person if that person is already suffering from some sort of cardiac problem. I think Alex did that to your mother. He used that mask to frighten her, hoping she would have a heart attack and die. He got lucky—she happened to be in her bath when it occurred, causing her to slip beneath the water and drown."

Philippa put a hand to her head. "This is terrible. Just terrible." She looked at Monica. "Have you told the police this?"

Monica sighed. "No. It's only a theory."

"That may be, but it makes perfect sense, don't you think?"

Chapter 19

Should she tell Detective Stevens about the African mask and what she'd deduced? Monica wondered as she and Teddy drove away from Philippa's house. If Kiran was actually innocent, it would cause him a lot of distress. And perhaps the police had already uncovered facts that led in a completely different direction. She would merely be causing an unnecessary distraction.

Her cell phone rang as she was feeding Teddy. She glanced at the number and groaned.

"Monica? It's Mom."

Monica stifled a sigh. "Yes, Mom?"

"We're all quite excited here. Some good news. We received a last-minute request from the Restful Haven funeral parlor. They're hosting a memorial for a client followed by a small reception and they're asking if we can deliver some baked goods to serve with the coffee. Apparently, the manager of the Cranberry Cove Inn told them about us. Mick, bless him, has managed to pull everything together—some cranberry muffins, a dozen scones and a cranberry orange streusel cake."

Their little baking enterprise was expanding, Monica thought. First a small chain of gourmet stores had started selling their cranberry salsa, then the Cranberry Cove Inn began ordering cranberry salsa as well as cranberry compote, and word must have spread because now Restful Haven was looking to them for baked goods. An idea began to percolate in her mind. She'd have to run it past Greg to see what he thought.

"Does Mick need any help?" Guilt settled in Monica's stomach like a heavy rock. She should be at the farm kitchen helping out. On the other hand, Teddy needed her too. She felt like a rubber band being pulled in opposite directions. Just so it didn't snap.

"We could use some help, dear. We'll watch Teddy for you if you wouldn't mind delivering the order."

"Sure," Monica said without hesitation. Maybe this errand would assuage some of her guilty feelings. "Teddy's been fed and should be good for another couple of hours." She glanced at the baby. "He looks ready to take a nap so he shouldn't be any trouble."

"That's marvelous. The order needs to be delivered pronto. I would take it myself but my car is in the shop and Janice gave me a lift this morning."

Monica ended the call with a feeling of purpose. She was needed. She had to admit, if only to herself, that she'd been a little hurt that the farm kitchen and store were running so well without her.

Teddy began kicking his feet as she tucked him into his carriage, and by the time they were within sight of the farm kitchen he'd managed to kick off both of his socks.

"Wonderful," Nancy exclaimed when Monica arrived. "Everything is ready to go." She bent over Teddy's carriage and smiled. Despite the carriage bouncing over the bumpy dirt path, his eyes had closed and he'd fallen asleep.

Janice joined Nancy and they both peeked into the carriage. "Bare feet! He could get hypothermia." She tsk-tsked as she retrieved his socks and put them back on him.

Monica found herself struggling not to scream. "It's not that cold out. I doubt he was in danger of developing hypothermia."

Janice's expression hardened. "You can't be too careful."

Fortunately, Mick chose that moment to arrive with a large box. "Here you go." He carried it over to the table. "One dozen cranberry muffins, a dozen scones and a cranberry orange cake with streusel topping." He ticked them off on his fingers. "Can you manage?"

"No problem." Monica hefted the box onto her hip. "I won't be long," she called over her shoulder as she went out the door.

The Restful Haven funeral parlor seemed to be doing a brisk business. A number of cars were already in the parking lot when Monica drove in. She found a vacant spot and retrieved the box of baked goods from the trunk of her car. A delicious aroma wafted from the contents and Monica's stomach grumbled. She was tempted to snitch one of the muffins.

As she walked up the winding path to the funeral parlor, she daydreamed about possible future plans for the farm's goods. In that moment it felt as if the sky was the limit.

She was once again greeted by a man in a black suit and tie, although this one was younger and sported an unhealthy pallor, as if he hadn't seen daylight in months. He eyed the box in Monica's arms.

"Is that for the Fisher memorial reception?" His voice was so low, she had to lean forward to hear.

Fisher? Monica searched her memory. Wasn't that Timmy's last name?

"Follow me." The young man began to silently glide down the hall, the rubber soles of his shoes soundless on the wood floor. Monica found herself tiptoeing lest her footsteps disturb the silence. A hush hung over the building like a thick cloud and she could hear a clock ticking on a walnut side table. They passed a visitation room where people were filing past the casket displayed at the front and a smaller room with a discreet sign that read *Family Room*.

He led Monica into a small room at the back of the funeral parlor where a lace curtain fluttered in the breeze from the partially opened window. A long table, covered in a white cloth and stacked with dessert plates and napkins, was pushed against one wall and a smaller table set with a coffee urn and cups and saucers was across from it.

Monica began to arrange the baked goods on the table. Fortunately, Mick had thought to include several disposable platters. She spent a few minutes fussing then stood back and studied the display, changing the positions of one or two things until she was finally satisfied.

She was about to pick up the now empty box when Candi Clawson walked into the room. The dark roots were showing in her hair and her short black dress hung on her as if she had lost weight since she'd purchased it. She'd eschewed her signature chandelier earrings and was instead wearing small gold studs.

"Oh," she said when Monica turned around. "I didn't expect to see you here."

"I delivered the food." Monica waved a hand at the display on the table.

"The funeral parlor said they would take care of it but I had no idea . . ." Candi bit her lip. "I thought this was the least I could do for Timmy. He has no family, or at least none that care about him."

Monica was about to leave when people began to file into the room. A young man wearing jeans, a plaid flannel shirt and clutching a Detroit Tigers baseball cap in his hands looked over the selection of baked goods but didn't take anything.

An older couple arrived shortly afterward, the woman leaning heavily on a cane while the man held her arm. They introduced themselves as Timmy's former neighbors. They made a beeline for Monica's cranberry goods and loaded up plates with cranberry muffins and slices of cake. A few armless chairs had been arranged against the two remaining walls and they shuffled over to them and sat down.

Candi was talking to them when another girl walked in. She looked to be in her twenties and was pretty in a girl-next-door sort of way. She had thick auburn hair brushed back from her forehead and a sprinkling of freckles across her nose. Candi turned around to see who the newcomer was and her jaw went slack.

She stood for a moment, tottering on her high heels, then launched herself at the new arrival.

"How dare you show up here." Her voice rose to a screech.

The older couple's heads shot up, momentarily distracted from the slices of cake they were eating.

The girl took a step backward. "I have every right to be here." Her voice grew stronger with each word and she raised her chin. "I loved Timmy and he loved me."

"He didn't love you." Candi's face was so red Monica began to worry. "He loved me. We were going to be married. We have a *son*."

"No." The girl put her hands on either side of her face. "That's not true. It can't be. Timmy never told me . . ."

Candi had begun to sob. "I knew he was cheating on me. He came home one night smelling of that perfume you always wear. He promised me it wouldn't happen again. That it didn't mean anything. That you meant nothing to him."

The girl reeled as if each of Candi's words was a slap.

The young man with the baseball cap looked poised to bolt out the door but the elderly couple seemed to be hanging on every word.

Monica found it quite interesting that Timmy had been cheating on Candi. Did Timmy keep his promise that it wouldn't happen again? Or had the affair continued despite what he'd promised Candi? It must have been a blow to Candi, who'd been picturing marriage and a home for their son.

Could it have angered her enough to contemplate committing murder? Someone had been in the car with Timmy when he was shot. And the chandelier earring the police had found in the passenger well of the car was like the ones Candi wore. It wasn't out of the question to assume that she had been the one sitting in the front seat of the car with Timmy. The question, though, was whether she was the one who had pulled the trigger?

The funeral parlor was hushed with only the low murmur of voices coming through the open doors. Monica tiptoed back down the hall, past the visitation room, the family room, the reception desk and finally out the front door. She paused for a moment on the walkway to take a deep breath. The atmosphere inside the funeral parlor had felt close and the smell of decaying lilies permeating the air had contributed to the sensation of claustrophobia. She held her face up to the sun, enjoying the feeling of warmth on her skin after the chill inside.

She'd nearly reached her car when she noticed a woman walking toward her. She looked familiar and as she got closer, Monica realized it was Stephanie, the receptionist at Johnny-on-the-Spot. Monica stopped and said hello when they were nearly abreast of each other.

Stephanie looked startled. She lowered her sunglasses and peered at Monica.

"I'm afraid I don't . . ."

"We met at Johnny-on-the-Spot when I went to check on an invoice for my stepmother."

Stephanie's face was blank then suddenly cleared. "Oh, now I remember." She rubbed her forehead. "You have to excuse me. I've been in a fog ever since the baby was born. He's still not sleeping through the night and it's beginning to get to me."

"I know how you feel. I have an infant myself."

Stephanie perked up. "Then you do know how I feel. My friends all seem to have forgotten what it's like with a newborn. Most of their children are already in school." She scratched at a stain on the front of her jacket.

"Are you here for Timmy Fisher?"

Stephanie looked slightly embarrassed. "Yeah. I didn't know him well but I kinda felt sorry for him, you know?" She shrugged. "He was a bit of a loner and I was afraid no one would show up." She gestured toward the funeral parlor. "Everyone deserves a good send-off, my father always used to say."

She glanced up sharply. "Now I remember you," she said as if it had suddenly occurred to her. "You were asking about the missing porta-potty. And we talked about how weird it was that Lou wasn't invoicing those two customers who were getting porta-potties every week. And you know what?" She poked Monica's arm. "I remember the one guy because he had such a weird name. Just one name. He must have changed it because I can't imagine his parents picked it out for him. I saw an ad in the *Cranberry Cove Chronicle* that he's opened a spa in Cranberry Cove. That's what brought it back. Kiran. His name was Kiran."

Now that was interesting, Monica thought as she drove back to the farm. Interesting, but what did it mean? What was Kiran doing with a weekly delivery of a porta-potty? And why wasn't Johnny-on-the-Spot charging him for it? Did it fit in with her theory that the porta-potties were being used to transport drugs?

She thought she had the answer and she thought she knew how to prove it.

• • •

"You want to do what?" Gina said when Monica phoned her. Monica could picture her expression, her filler-enhanced lips curved into an astonished round *O*. There was a long pause before Gina spoke again. "Soul Spring Spa does have a class tonight. I think you'll like it. It's VR."

Monica frowned. "I'm almost afraid to ask. What's VR?" *Could it be even worse than crawling around on the floor making animal sounds?*

"Virtual Reality. You wear these special goggles and you do cardio routines in a virtual landscape like the jungle or outer space."

Would they be crawling around on the floor and making animal sounds but in a virtual jungle this time?

"I think you'll like it."

Monica didn't know about that but it didn't matter. It suited her purpose so she'd do it.

"Okay, I'm game."

"Good for you. I'll pick you up at six forty-five. Greg should be home by then and he can look after Teddy." Monica was about to end the call when Gina said, "Oh, and be sure to wear dark clothing."

Chapter 20

Even though Monica thought Gina was being overly dramatic, she managed to scrounge up a pair of black leggings and a black T-shirt. At least it was mostly black—*Save the Whales* was written across the front in white lettering.

"What is it going to be this time?" Greg patted Teddy's back as he lay on his shoulder. "Hula-Hoops? Jump ropes?"

Monica grimaced. "Something called virtual reality cardio."

"Good luck," Greg called as Monica headed out the door to the driveway, where Gina's Mercedes was purring impatiently.

Gina looked her over. "I thought you were going to wear black?"

"I am." Monica pointed at her T-shirt. "See?"

"But the writing on it is white. Seriously. Save the Whales?" Gina stepped on the gas and they shot down the driveway.

Monica was half hoping there'd be a reason to avoid going to the spa—a road closure, sudden power outage . . . anything. What had she been thinking when she'd cooked up this scheme? She hadn't been. Thinking. That was the problem.

Despite Monica's prayers, they arrived at Soul Spring Spa on time and more or less in one piece, although she was slightly shaken and stirred by Gina's driving.

Kiran was at the door to welcome them wearing safari garb—sand-colored cargo pants, a camouflage campaign shirt and a pair of lace-up boots. He handed out the virtual reality headsets and they filed into the exercise room, taking their places around the floor.

Monica thought the headsets made them look like a group of snorkelers. Just so there weren't any sharks.

The class began and Monica found herself in a startlingly real jungle landscape where she was being forced to run uphill through knee-high grasses. Suddenly a very realistic-looking lion appeared, roared loudly and began to salivate at the sight of her. She ran faster. A coiled snake reared up out of the swaying grasses and hissed at her. Her heartbeat took a leap forward and sweat was beginning to pour down her face. She was quite sure she jumped ten feet in the air when Gina tapped her on the shoulder.

She ripped off her headset, put her hands on her knees and

panted, frantically trying to take in enough oxygen.

"Let's go," Gina whispered.

Monica was more than willing to comply. She glanced at Kiran. He was at the front of the class pretending to box with a predator. She had to stifle a laugh as she and Gina slipped from the room.

"Let's look in his office first."

Gina led the way and Monica followed. She half expected to see a wild animal jump out of the shadows at her. She was beginning to wonder if her plan to steal a bottle of the powdered Thermodynamics was a good idea. What if the analysis showed it was a completely harmless, if also useless, substance made up of various herbal supplements?

There was no going back now. Gina was already opening the door to the office closet and riffling through the cabinet. She held her hands out. "Nothing. But there are other places to look."

She and Monica inched their way down the hall, where they could hear the huffing and puffing of the women still struggling through a virtual jungle in the exercise room.

There was a noise at the end of the hall and Monica stifled a yelp. She was trying to come up with an explanation for sneaking around when she realized no one was there. She put a hand to her chest. That had gotten her heart rate up even higher than the exercise class had.

"There's a storeroom back here." Gina opened a door, felt along the wall and flicked on the light. She motioned to Monica. "Quick," and shut the door behind her.

The room was stuffed with cartons of Thermodynamics along with exercise equipment, like the Hula-Hoops they'd used in class.

They began going through the cartons one by one. Several were stacked on top of each other and Monica was getting a workout lifting them and then putting them back. So far all they'd found were boxes of Thermodynamics capsules—no powder. Maybe Monica's theory wasn't valid after all?

"What now?" Gina stood with her hands on her hips.

"There's one last place we can look. But it's going to be dicey."

Gina rubbed her hands together. "Let's go."

"Put on your headset." Monica led them back to the exercise room, where the class was still struggling through the workout. Fortunately, they were all focused on virtual reality instead of reality and no one noticed as Monica and Gina slunk past them and opened the door to the closet at the far end.

They didn't dare turn on the light. They'd left the door cracked and would have to search by the shaft of light shining through. Monica found herself going through things by touch. The first box she opened contained towels. She grabbed one and mopped up the perspiration from her forehead and then draped it around her neck. She continued her search and found a carton of hand sanitizer, one of rolls of toilet paper and finally she hit the jackpot. Bottles of Thermodynamics. She gave one a shake and listened for the rattle of capsules. Nothing.

She held the bottle up to the light coming through the partially open door and Gina had to shush her when she nearly yelled in excitement.

"We've got it."

Gina glanced at her watch. "We'd better hurry. Class is almost over."

Suddenly, all the participants began whipping their masks off and reaching for their water bottles.

"Quick! Hide the bottle."

Monica stared at it helplessly before finally shoving it under her T-shirt. "I look like I've sprouted a hernia."

"Never mind that," Gina hissed. "We have to get out of here."

The class was over and everyone was placing their virtual reality headsets in a box Kiran had provided. Monica hunched over trying to hide the bulge under her T-shirt as she placed hers in with the others.

Kiran was at the entrance to the room bowing to everyone as they left, his hands folded as if in prayer.

He put out a hand to stop Monica and Gina as they prepared to leave.

"Did you enjoy the class?"

His breathy, sibilant voice washed over Monica and made her shiver. And the way he looked her over, his glance resting on the bottle hidden beneath her Save the Whales T-shirt, made her stomach clench.

Finally, they were out the door and nearly running for Gina's car.

"Who are we going to get to analyze the stuff in that bottle?" Gina started the car and backed out of the parking space, narrowly missing a lamppost.

Monica hadn't thought that far ahead. "I don't know. Probably the best thing to do is to deliver it to Detective Stevens and let her handle it."

It wasn't until Gina had dropped her off that Monica took the towel from around her neck. She'd wash it and return it to Soul Spring Spa. Preferably via Gina. She wasn't sure she'd survive any more of Kiran's exercise classes. And the look he'd given her when she left the spa had given her the chills.

• • •

As soon as Teddy was changed and fed Monica headed out. The day was overcast with swift clouds moving in across the lake. She quickly glanced into the rearview mirror and was relieved to see that her umbrella was still in the backseat where she'd stashed it the last time she'd used it.

The parking lot at the police station wasn't full and she found a spot quite near the entrance. It was only a few feet from her car to the overhang that protected the front door and she decided to leave her umbrella in the car.

She put a drowsy Teddy in the sling and carried him inside.

The officer at the front desk immediately stood up and peered at Teddy over the desk. He had gray hair cut close to his scalp and his stomach pushed against the confines of his shirt.

"The wife and I are expecting our first grandchild," he said, puffing his chest out proudly. "Our daughter's having a boy. I had a feeling that was what it was going to be and they had one of those ultrasounds and confirmed it. I can't wait to take the little sprout to the park to throw a ball around." The dreamy look left his face and he snapped to. "How can I help you?"

"I was hoping to see Detective Stevens."

He smiled. "You're in luck. She just got back and is in her office." He crooked a finger at her. "Follow me."

Monica had been to Stevens's office before but it appeared to have been moved. The new space was equally cramped with what looked like the same stacks of papers threatening to totter off the desk.

Stevens looked weary. Even her white blouse was sagging, the collar limp. Her eyes were expressionless as she looked at Monica. She gestured to the bag in Monica's hand.

"Please tell me that's a large double-strength coffee and something to eat."

"I hate to disappoint you." Monica removed the bottle of Thermodynamics and placed it on Stevens's desk.

Stevens picked it up and glanced at the label. "For energy, vitality and youthfulness," she read. "Is this for me? I could certainly use energy, vitality and youthfulness. I'm dead tired and I feel a thousand years old."

Monica took a deep breath. "There's a lot to explain."

Stevens leaned back in her chair and folded her arms behind her head. "Try me." She stifled a yawn. "Sorry. My son is still having nightmares, which means I can't sleep either."

Monica smoothed Teddy's hair. "We're almost sleeping all night. I'm beginning to feel human again."

"So, what is this you've brought me?" Stevens tapped the bottle with her index finger.

"Drugs." Monica gulped. "At least I think so. You know that porta-potty that was found in the field that had traces of drugs in it?"

Stevens nodded.

"It all relates to that. At least I think so." Suddenly she doubted her own theory. Was she trying to jam random facts together to create a solution to the mystery? Where to begin?

The beginning is always a good place, she reminded herself.

"Johnny-on-the-Spot was being used to distribute drugs."

"Yes. We caught the owner, Lou King, red-handed receiving a shipment of pure, uncut cocaine. Tell me something I don't know."

"Lou was distributing the cocaine stashed in his porta-potties."

Stevens sat upright and the back of her chair sprang forward. "You're kidding." She made a face. "Ewww. I guess people who take drugs aren't too particular about where they come from."

"Lou's secretary told me that he regularly sent a porta-potty to each of two customers but he never billed them for the rental. I think the drugs were secreted inside."

Stevens massaged the back of her neck. "And I suppose those customers"—she put the word in air quotes—"then cut the cocaine and passed it along to the next person in the chain. But what does that have to do with . . ." She glanced at the jar on her desk. "Thermodynamics?"

"My stepmother is selling Thermodynamics for the Soul Spring Spa."

Stevens rolled her eyes. "Sounds like a scam. I'm sure we'll be getting complaints about it soon enough."

"The legitimate jars of Thermodynamics contain various supplements in capsules, but I discovered some that contain powder instead. I think the powder includes cocaine."

Stevens's eyebrows shot up. "It's worth having it tested."

"According to Lou's secretary, one of the customers receiving deliveries of the porta-potties on a regular basis was Alex Timmerman. He goes by the name Kiran now and is the owner of the Soul Spring Spa."

Teddy began to stir and Monica rocked back and forth to soothe him back to sleep.

"I think Kiran is doctoring the cocaine. Or whatever it is you call it."

"Cutting. He's cutting the cocaine with another substance."

"Okay, he's cutting the cocaine, packing it in Thermodynamics bottles and distributing it to the next person in line." She patted Teddy's back. "I've been thinking about it. Where did he get the money to open his spa? As far as I can tell, he'd been working as a home health aide for a hospice company."

"Not an easy way to make money." Stevens stifled another yawn.

"True. Selling cocaine is a lot easier."

Stevens pulled a plastic bag from her desk drawer and dropped the container of Thermodynamics into it. "If this tests out, I'll be having a word with Mr. Timmerman."

Chapter 21

Monica wasn't sure how she felt when she left Stevens's office. She thought Stevens had taken her theory seriously but perhaps she'd only been humoring her? Either way, she'd done what she felt was right.

She hadn't been prepared to share with Stevens what she'd learned about Kiran supposedly stealing from his patients. Her evidence was too vague. Once she knew more, she'd lay it all out and let the police handle the rest.

She was on her way to her car when someone called her name. She spun around but didn't immediately see anyone.

"Over here." A window buzzed down and a hand waved. Candi was sitting in her car, leaning out the driver's window.

Monica walked over and bent down. It was obvious Candi had been crying. Her skin was blotchy and her eyes swollen.

"I need to talk to you. Can you help me?"

"What is it?" Monica shaded her eyes against the sun glancing off the roof of Candi's car.

"Why don't you get in."

Monica reluctantly went around the car, opened the passenger door and carefully slid into the seat. She could tell by Teddy's movements that he wasn't going to be content in the sling for long.

Candi had the radio playing—some mournful country and western song—and she reached out a hand and switched it off.

"The police want to question me about Timmy's death." She blurted the words out suddenly.

"I'm sure it's only routine."

Candi sniffed loudly. "I don't know what to tell them."

"You could start with the truth." Teddy would need feeding soon and Monica was anxious to get home. She wished Candi would get to the point.

"I'm afraid they won't believe me." Candi swiped a hand across her nose.

"If it's the truth, there will be proof." Candi moaned. "Why don't you tell me what happened?"

"I was in the car with Timmy the day he was shot." She hiccoughed.

"We had a . . . a fight. I knew he was cheating on me even though he insisted it wasn't true."

Monica thought back to Timmy's memorial service and the girl who had shown up and upset Candi.

"I was so mad. I guess I did something foolish. I told him to stop and let me out of the car." She pulled a tissue out of the sleeve of her sweater and blew her nose. "I figured I could hitch a ride home easily enough."

She twisted around in her seat to face Monica. "I was halfway across that field when I sort of figured I'd made a stupid mistake. Those weeds were scratching my legs and I was already out of breath. Timmy was still parked by the side of the road. I guess he was counting on me changing my mind."

"Then what happened?" Monica prompted.

"Another car pulled up in back of Timmy. Even from a distance I could tell it was an expensive car, quiet and sleek. I think it was an Audi. Dark black." Candi giggled briefly. "I don't suppose there's any other kind of black, is there."

Monica assumed that wasn't meant to be a question.

"A man got out. He looked familiar but I didn't know why." She turned to Monica. "He'd been at your brother's wedding. He'd shaved his head and was dressing kind of weird but I realized it was someone my mother used to work with at Loving Hands Hospice."

"Do you remember his name?"

Candi shook her head. "I don't. But I'm pretty sure it was him."

So, Kiran had worked with Jolie. Monica had suspected as such. Was he the same employee who was fired because of her?

"Then what happened?"

"He got in the car with Timmy."

"Were they arguing?"

"I couldn't tell. But then I heard a shot . . ." Candi covered her face with her hands. "I didn't know what to do. What if he saw me? I dropped to the ground hoping the grasses would hide me and I waited while the man got out of Timmy's car and back into his own. I didn't stand up until I heard him pull away."

"Timmy had been shot in the head. Did you see him leave the car and stagger up the hill?"

"No." Candi whimpered. "I had my eyes shut tight like you do when you're a little kid and you're scared." She squirmed in her seat. "I know I should have done something to help Timmy but I panicked. I ran the rest of the way across the field until I came to a road. The first person that came by—a guy in a red pickup truck—gave me a lift."

"You have to tell the police all that."

"What if they don't believe me? They'll think I did it."

Candi began to cry again and Teddy let out a wail as if to join her in the chorus.

Monica reached for the door handle. "Detective Stevens is very easy to talk to. There's no need to worry. Now I have to go." She patted Candi's arm and got out of the car.

• • •

Teddy was down for his nap and Monica was fixing herself lunch. She'd turned some leftover chicken into chicken salad with mayonnaise, chopped walnuts and dried cranberries. She dished out a scoop of it, placed it on a bed of lettuce and carried it to the table. She was about to sit down when she remembered she needed to throw a load of clothes in the washing machine. Teddy was nearly out of clean onesies. She couldn't believe how many garments a tiny baby could manage to soil in just two or three days.

She went through the things in the laundry basket one by one, looking for stains and spraying them with stain remover. She reached for the final item and paused. It was a napkin she didn't recognize. Where did it come from and how did it get in her laundry basket?

She smacked her forehead with her palm. It was the towel she'd picked up at Soul Spring Spa, although now she could see it wasn't a towel but a napkin.

Why would Kiran need napkins at his spa? She doubted he was hosting dinner parties there. She examined it more closely. It was the same shade as the ones used at Jeff and Lauren's wedding. She looked more closely and noticed a slash of crimson lipstick in one corner.

For one silly moment she pictured Kiran with red lips. The vision made her laugh. She was about to toss the napkin in the washer—the least she could do was return it clean—when a thought occurred to her. The medical examiner had said Jolie had been suffocated with something. Could it have been a napkin? Could that lipstick stain have been from her?

• • •

"Can I help?" Greg said as Monica began peeling potatoes. Teddy was in his baby seat, his eyes beginning to track their movements. It seemed to amuse him because he kicked his feet in excitement.

Monica put the peeler down and leaned against the kitchen counter. How to explain it all to Greg?

"I grabbed what I thought was a towel when I went to Soul Spring Spa with Gina and inadvertently brought it home with me. I was about to throw it in the wash when I got a better look at it and realized it was actually a napkin."

"A napkin?" Greg looked puzzled.

"There's lipstick on it," she added somewhat sheepishly. "I recognized it as one of the napkins used at my brother's wedding. It's the same shade of pink . . ."

"Oh?" Greg began setting the table.

Monica tried to put her thoughts in order. "Jolie Spencer was suffocated, right? The medical examiner concluded that something had been held against her face . . . her mouth . . . to smother her."

"I understand where you're going with this but couldn't that napkin have belonged to anyone? Most of the women at the wedding were wearing lipstick."

"But why would Kiran have taken it?"

Greg shrugged. "I don't know. People are known for walking off with the strangest things. Silverware from restaurants is a popular one. Micky occasionally complains about that. And back when everyone smoked it was ashtrays. And now hotels have signs up warning against stealing the terry-cloth bathrobes." He plunked down forks and knives. "He might have picked it up and absentmindedly stuffed it in his pocket and forgotten about it."

Monica felt slightly deflated, although she was convinced it all added up. But did it add up enough for her to go to Stevens with it?

• • •

Monica checked the weather report the next morning as she changed Teddy. The forecast called for an unseasonably warm day with plenty of sunshine. She glanced out the window. It would do them both good to get some fresh air. She decided she would put Teddy in the baby sling and take a walk along the lakeshore.

It had been a good idea, Monica thought as she got Teddy out of his car seat and nestled him in the sling on her chest. His breathing was even, he was already asleep.

The sand felt good on her bare feet and the sun was warm on her face and back. The beach was nearly deserted. Seagulls were squabbling over something one of them had dug up in the sand, pecking at each other and occasionally taking flight to swoop down at a different angle.

A speck in the distance slowly came into focus and Monica realized it was a girl sitting in the sand. She'd drawn her knees into her chest and had hunched over, wrapping her arms around them. Her back was heaving and Monica realized she was crying.

She looked up when Monica's shadow fell across the sand in front of her. Monica realized it was the young woman who had appeared at Timmy's memorial service and had upset Candi.

"Is there anything I can do?" Monica said softly.

The girl sniffed and looked up. "Oh. You're the woman who was at Timmy's memorial service, aren't you?"

"Yes." Monica sank down and sat cross-legged on the sand.

"You knew Timmy?"

Monica hesitated. "Not well."

"We were in love. We started out as friends. We met at the gym. He used to tease me about how slowly I was running on the treadmill. I wasn't. I was ranked at the top for the hundred-meter sprint when I was in college. He was obviously only kidding me. He had a good sense of humor." She smiled and a dimple appeared in her cheek. "He asked me if I wanted to go for a smoothie. We started talking and well . . ." She shrugged. "One thing led to another. We didn't plan for it to happen."

She dug her toes into the sand. "He promised me he was going to tell Candi very soon so we could be together. But Candi found out before he had the chance." She looked at Monica, her mouth drawn down. "She turned up at my apartment and said she was going to kill

Timmy. She even showed me the gun she had in her purse."

Monica tried to hide her surprise. "What did you do?"

"I texted Timmy right away. Told him to be careful. But I don't know if he ever saw my text. Or maybe he just didn't believe me." She covered her face with her hands.

"Do you really think Candi would have killed Timmy?"

"Who knows. She was acting crazy, waving that gun around. She said she knew how to use it and nothing was going to stop her."

• • •

Teddy had been fed and seemed to be content in his carry cot, staring at the brightly colored mobile hanging over him and attempting to kick it. Monica spent the precious time packing a few more boxes. She felt betwixt and between. Slowly, they were taking apart the cottage she'd lived in and loved for several years and yet they hadn't made a home out of their new house yet. She sat back on her haunches and thought about it—all that space!

It was time to hand the cottage over to Jeff and Lauren, she reminded herself. She was confident they would love it as much as she did. Lauren had already shared a few of her plans for decorating it and Monica knew she was anxious to move in.

She peeked into Teddy's carry cot and saw that his eyelids were fluttering closed. Good. That would give her a bit more time to pack.

She jumped when someone knocked on the back door and dropped the vase she was holding. It hit the floor and shattered. Monica groaned. It had been a wedding present from Bart and his wife. Fortunately, it was unlikely they'd ever find out what had happened to it.

She dashed into the kitchen before the person could knock again and wake Teddy.

"Gina!"

Gina burst into the room in her usual fashion bringing with her some dried leaves that had stuck to her shoes. Mittens appeared and began to bat at one of them.

Gina bent down to pet Hercule. "Kiran is offering an exciting new class today."

"No."

Gina crossed her arms over her chest. "You haven't even heard what it is yet."

"I don't care. Besides, I think Kiran is suspicious of us. If he really is involved in selling drugs, it could be dangerous."

Gina waved a hand in the air, her bright orange nails flashing in the sunlight spilling through the kitchen window.

"And if we don't show up again, he'll think we're on to him. Besides, he's done wonders for my figure." Gina swept a hand down her body, which was encased in fuchsia leggings and a matching midriff-baring top.

Monica didn't notice much of a difference but she thought she'd better keep that to herself.

"The class will be fantastic. You'll love it."

"What is it?" Monica was curious in spite of herself. How could you possibly beat crawling around like an animal or spinning a Hula-Hoop for an hour?

"It's doga."

"What on earth is that?"

"It's yoga with your dog. We could bring Hercule." At the sound of his name, Hercule's ears perked up.

"I can't just leave Teddy here alone." Sometimes Monica wondered how Jeff had survived infancy with a mother like Gina.

"Call that woman you've hired as a nanny. See if she's willing to sit with Teddy for a couple of hours."

"I'll be leaving Teddy soon enough when I go back to work in the farm kitchen."

"You can't spend every minute with him. Besides, all babies really do at this stage is eat and sleep." Gina's smile was smug. "Besides, who knows what else we might uncover?"

Gina knew her well, Monica thought. "Oh, alright. I'll give Alice a call."

Alice was thrilled when Monica rang her and said she'd be right over.

"Go." Gina gave Monica a playful shove. "Put your exercise clothes on."

Monica was pulling on her leggings when Alice arrived. She quickly yanked her hair back into a ponytail and hurried downstairs.

Alice had taken Teddy from his carry cot and was carrying him around the living room pointing out different things. Teddy was mostly oblivious but occasionally his eyes tracked Alice's pointing finger.

"Oh," she said to Monica. "I remembered the name of that fellow who frequently worked with Jolie. "It was Alan or Alex or something with an *A* and his last name was Timmerman."

Chapter 22

Kiran was trying to kill her.

Her hamstrings were protesting and her arms were shaking. Hercule licked her face in sympathy as if he understood her difficulty trying to maintain Adho Mukha Savasana, or Downward Facing Dog Pose. Kiran was at the head of the class urging them to keep their heels on the floor.

A golden retriever was actually doing the pose along with its owner while a West Highland white terrier had wandered off to sniff the corners of the room. One of the dogs began to bark and the others immediately joined it. It was pandemonium.

Monica couldn't have been more relieved when the class was finally over.

Kiran sprang up from Savasana, or Corpse Pose, which they'd been practicing.

"Brava, ladies. That was wonderful." He looked slightly alarmed when a dog of indeterminate breed went over to sniff him. "I'll bring out towels for everyone." He scampered off toward the closet.

Gina wiped a hand across her brow. "Who knew yoga could be so strenuous." She looked around. "I thought Kiran was getting us towels. Do you think he collapsed from all those cobra and cow poses he had us do?"

Towels. Monica drew in a breath. She felt a flush rise from her neck to her face and it wasn't because of the yoga. What if Kiran noticed that the napkin that had been on top of the box of towels was missing? Would he suspect them?

"I'll see what he's doing." Monica headed in the direction of the storage closet.

She found Kiran frantically searching through the stacked boxes. Towels were strewn across the floor and the contents of a drawer had been tipped out.

Monica tiptoed away. He must be looking for the napkin she'd taken. What else could have him in such a panic?

She had to have been right about the napkin. It had to have been the one Kiran had used to suffocate Jolie.

• • •

Monica put the bouncing baby seat Nora had given them in the bathroom and settled Teddy in it. He kicked his legs and was thrilled when it bounced slightly. She took a quick shower, occasionally peering around the shower curtain to check on Teddy. She was surprised at how much of a sweat she'd worked up in the yoga class. Weren't they supposed to be calming and peaceful? Even Hercule was collapsed in the corner, his pink tongue hanging out the side of his mouth.

She was drying off when her cell phone rang. It was Mick and he sounded upset. He said he wanted to talk to her in person.

Monica felt her stomach clench. He wasn't going to tell her he was quitting, was he? She dried off quickly and got dressed. She changed Teddy's diaper, put his jacket on him and strapped him into his carriage.

Her thoughts were whirling in circles as she pushed the carriage down the dirt path, swerving now and then to avoid the worst of the potholes. Her heart was beating abnormally fast and she told herself to calm down. It was probably nothing. Perhaps Mick had come up with an idea for a new product. He'd done that before and his cranberry cookies with white chocolate chunks had been a huge success. She was probably worrying for no reason.

She paused outside the door to the farm kitchen then resolutely reached for the door handle and turned it.

Mick was alone in the kitchen, spraying the counters with cleaning solution and wiping them down. The ovens were off and all the bakeware was washed and put away. He stopped what he was doing when he saw Monica.

"How's Teddy?" He came out from behind the counter. "Getting big, yeah?"

Monica bit her tongue. Her instinct was to burst out with *What did you want to talk to me about?* Instead, they spent a few moments admiring Teddy to ease the tension.

Mick's eyes turned dark and his expression somber. "I have a problem. I don't know if you can help me." His hand was in his pocket and he was playing with something. He noticed Monica looking.

"Komboloi. Worry beads." He pulled a circular string of green agate stones from his pocket.

"What's worrying you?" Teddy began to fuss and Monica moved the carriage back and forth to soothe him.

Mick massaged his temples with his fingers. "I don't know where to begin."

Monica waited patiently.

"It's about Candi. Jolie's daughter. She thinks I have money . . . money from her mother."

So, he wasn't going to tell her he was quitting. Monica's shoulders relaxed and she unclenched her teeth. Her jaw had started to ache.

"Candi wants money? From you?"

Mick nodded.

"Can't you say no? Tell her you don't have any?" The solution seemed simple enough to Monica.

"She's . . . what do you call it? Blackmailing me."

"Blackmailing! How? Why?" Monica's head had begun to spin.

"She knows I'm not supposed to be here. I suppose Jolie told her. I came here on a tourist visa and it ended a long time ago. She's threatening to report me to immigration and have me deported." He ducked his head. "I admit that I married Jolie so I could stay in this country. She knew I didn't love her. But she wanted a companion. She didn't like being alone. She had money and she'd said we'd travel. And I would eventually get my green card." He stared off into the distance. "I was good to her. At least I can say that."

He went silent and looked at Monica.

"Does Candi need money?"

Mick scratched the back of his neck. "Yeah. Her mother was giving her an allowance. Enough to live on and then some. And she seems to think Jolie gave me money but she didn't. She doesn't want to believe me."

"And then her mother died. Obviously, the payments must have stopped." Monica jiggled the carriage handle.

Mick shook his head. "No, it wasn't then. It was before Jolie died. Candi and Jolie had a fight and Jolie said she wasn't going to give her any more money. I heard them arguing. Candi was furious. She said her mother owed her."

"Do you know what they fought about?"

"It had something to do with the guy Candi was dating. Jolie said that if Candi continued to see him, she would cut off Candi's allowance."

"Do you know who this boyfriend was?"

"No. But it sounded like Candi had known him a long time."

That had to have been Timmy, Monica thought. Jolie hadn't liked him the first time Candi had dated him and obviously that hadn't changed. She'd made sure the relationship couldn't continue by calling the police on Timmy, and this time she was using money to control her daughter and put an end to the romance.

The best thing for her to do was to help Mick begin the process of getting a work visa.

Mick's hand was in his pocket nervously fingering his worry beads. "What should I do?"

"I'm going to put in an application for you to get a temporary work visa as my employee. After that, we'll have to see. An immigration lawyer will be able to tell us if you can still get a green card."

Mick's face had begun to clear and the hand in his pocket stilled.

"I'll do it right away. You'll have to find a way to stall Candi meanwhile."

• • •

"Let's go see Auntie Nora," Monica said to Teddy as she wheeled the carriage in the direction of the farm store.

Monica noticed the parking lot was empty when it came into view. She glanced at her phone. Of course, it was nearly closing time.

A bell jangled when she pushed open the door to the store. "Look who's come to say hello."

Nora let out a squeal. "How is that little guy. I bet he's grown since the last time I saw him." She leaned over the carriage and made cooing noises.

"He does seem to grow a bit every day. His newborn onesies are already too small."

"Let's have a cup of coffee." Nora bustled over to the coffee maker and began fussing with some mugs with *Sassamanash Farm* written on them in cranberry red. She pointed at the door. "Can you change the sign to closed?"

Monica flipped it over and parked Teddy's carriage by one of the tables. She lifted him out and cradled him in her arms while he tried to put his hand in his mouth.

Nora brought two mugs of coffee to the table and sat down. "How is Greg?"

"He's well. Excited about moving into our new house."

"I can imagine." Nora blew on her coffee. "Careful. It's hot." She took a sip. "How are the newlyweds doing? Enjoying married life?"

"Yes, I think so. They certainly seem happy."

"Living with someone takes some getting used to. It takes a few years to be completely comfortable and eventually you couldn't imagine life without your spouse. If you're lucky, that is." She put her cup down. "It was such a lovely wedding." Her expression turned somber. "Until the end, that is."

"Fortunately, Jeff and Lauren had already left by then."

"Yes." Nora stared into her coffee. "They still haven't found the killer, have they?"

Monica shook her head.

"I need your opinion on something. On whether or not I should tell Detective Stevens this. It might not be important but just in case it is . . ."

Monica raised her eyebrows.

"I remember seeing that woman who was murdered arguing with a young woman. She was wearing these outrageous earrings—long and dangly. They would have driven me crazy." She made a face. "Anyway, that poor woman who was killed got up from her table and headed toward the porta-potties. But then that girl who had been arguing with her got up too and followed her."

"To the porta-potties?"

"Yes. In that direction anyway." She ran a finger around the rim of her coffee mug. "Do you think I should tell Detective Stevens that? I don't want to get the poor girl in trouble when all she wanted to do was use the uh, facilities."

"I think you should tell her. She'll know whether it means anything or not."

Nora's face cleared. "Thanks. I'll phone her after I close up."

So, Candi had followed her mother to the porta-potties. For an innocent reason or to continue their argument? And had their argument gotten out of hand?

But then why did Kiran hide that napkin? Had he absentmindedly stuck it in his pocket as Greg had suggested?

None of it made any sense. Monica hoped Stevens would have more luck unraveling this than she was.

• • •

"It's a lovely evening," Greg said as he carried the dinner dishes to the sink. "Let's go get an ice cream."

"But Teddy . . ."

"He's been fed, changed and can sleep in his carriage."

Hercule looked at them expectantly.

"Sorry, bud." Greg scratched the dog's ears. "No dogs are allowed in the ice cream parlor."

Greg took Hercule for a quick walk while Monica got Teddy ready and then they were off.

It almost felt like a date, Monica thought as they drove along the lake and the sun began its descent in the sky, leaving behind bold streaks of red, orange and pink. She stifled a laugh. Except for the baby in the backseat, of course.

They parked in front of the drugstore, transferred a sleeping Teddy to his carriage and strolled down the street. The Golden Scoop was crowded so Greg offered to stay outside with Teddy as long as Monica got him a double butter pecan cone.

The Golden Scoop was decorated in the style of a nineteen-fifties ice cream parlor with red leather booths, a long counter lined with swivel stools with red leather seats and a shiny stainless steel milkshake machine whirring behind the counter. Monica inhaled the scent of vanilla and sugar and was immediately transported back to her childhood, when her father would take her to the ice cream parlor in her hometown.

She joined the line at the take-out counter and glanced at the menu board considering her choices. She usually got chocolate chip mint but she thought she'd try the salted caramel this time.

The line moved slowly and Monica amused herself by watching the patrons reflected in the large round mirror behind the take-out counter. She was surprised to see Candi Clawson sitting in one of the booths digging into a hot fudge sundae. She was even more surprised when Kiran suddenly slipped into the booth opposite her. The look on Candi's face made it clear she hadn't invited him nor expected him. Monica didn't even realize they knew each other.

She managed to sidle closer to where they were sitting and pick up snatches of their conversation.

"I don't have the money." Candi was near tears.

"You'd better get it then."

"What am I supposed to do? My mother's gone and there's no money."

"What about that guy Mick? He must be rolling in it. Surely, he doesn't want you to report him to immigration. He can't spend the money if he's in jail."

"He claims he doesn't have any money. After my mother died, all of it went to those wretched Spencer girls. If you knew how they'd treated me . . ."

"That's beside the point," Kiran snapped. "Do you want me to go to the police?"

Monica heard Candi gasp and could easily imagine the look on her face. But what was Kiran talking about? The police? Did Kiran think Candi had killed Timmy or did he know she had?

"I have the napkin, remember?"

So this wasn't about Timmy. Monica knew Kiran was bluffing. *She* had the napkin and planned to take it to Detective Stevens in the morning.

"What is the napkin going to tell the police, anyway?"

Kiran gave a laugh that wasn't in the least bit humorous. "Have you never seen a crime drama on television or at the movies? DNA, that's what the police will find. Yours and your dead mother's. And they'll finally know who killed Jolie Spencer."

Monica made a small noise like a squeak and hoped they hadn't heard her.

"You wouldn't . . ."

Kiran said something in a low voice that Monica couldn't hear.

"What can I get you?" the young man behind the counter said, startling Monica.

She hesitated. "Uh, two cones, one double scoop butter pecan and one single salted caramel."

"Coming right up."

Monica listened intently but she couldn't hear any more of Candi's and Kiran's conversation. She risked a quick glance behind her. It looked as if Kiran had left. Candi had pushed her sundae to the side. Obviously, the conversation had made her lose her appetite.

She barely remembered being handed the two ice cream cones and paying for them. So Candi had murdered her mother, not Kiran. Kiran was obviously using the napkin to blackmail her.

Had Candi killed Timmy as well? What was that saying of her grandmother's—in for a penny, in for a pound. Candi had already committed murder and had nothing to lose by pulling the trigger on her boyfriend.

Chapter 23

Monica was relieved when the door to the Golden Scoop closed behind her. Candi had spotted her on her way out and the look she'd given Monica had been so chilling she'd nearly dropped the two cones.

Did Candi know she'd overheard hers and Kiran's conversation?

"Watch out, it's dripping," Greg said as Monica handed him his scoops of butter pecan. He looked at her. "What's the matter? You look like something scared you."

"Nothing. I . . . I almost dropped the cones on my way out, that's all." Her ice cream was rapidly melting and running down her hand.

"You'd better start eating that." Greg nodded at the cone.

On the way home, Monica's thoughts went around and around and she barely noticed the passing scenery. All she could think about was getting the napkin out of the house and taking it to Detective Stevens.

"You're awfully quiet," Greg said, glancing at her.

"I overheard something that disturbed me. Candi Clawson was in one of the booths near the take-out counter. She was talking to Kiran—the fellow who owns the Soul Spring Spa."

"The one Gina likes so much?"

"Yes. Kiran accused Candi of murdering her mother and Candi didn't deny it."

"I think you should tell the police that. Let them sort it out."

"I will. I'm going to call Detective Stevens as soon as we get home and I get Teddy settled."

• • •

Teddy needed to be changed and fed when they got home, and by the time Monica had him down for the night, it was almost eight o'clock. She tiptoed out of his bedroom and down the stairs. She poured herself a glass of water and took it to the kitchen table.

Since this wasn't an emergency requiring immediate assistance, she didn't dial 911 but rather the number for the police station.

A deep, authoritative-sounding voice answered, "Cranberry Cove Police Department."

"I'd like to speak to Detective Stevens, please. This is Monica Albertson calling."

"I'm afraid Detective Stevens isn't in at the moment. Would you like to leave a message? If this is an emergency . . ."

"No, no, it's not." Monica hesitated. "Can you ask her to call me?" She gave him her cell phone number.

"That's Monica Albertson. correct?"

"Yes."

"I'll see that she gets the message."

• • •

Stevens still hadn't called by the next morning. Monica kept staring at her cell phone as if willing it to ring. She could call and leave another message. Or, she could drive down to the police station and deliver the suspicious napkin at the same time.

Greg was heading to an estate sale later in the morning and agreed to watch Teddy while she was gone.

Monica placed the lipstick-stained napkin in a plastic bag, carried it out to her car and put it on the passenger seat next to her.

There was little traffic and it wasn't long before she arrived at the police station. Stevens was eating a bagel when Monica was shown into her office.

"I didn't mean to disturb your breakfast . . ."

"Breakfast? This? A stale bagel and cold coffee? Don't worry about it." She pushed aside the piece of wax paper with the half-eaten bagel on it. "We've been so busy I haven't had the time to eat properly."

"If I'd known, I would have brought you some cranberry muffins."

"My mouth is watering." She gestured toward the bag in Monica's hand. "It looks like you did bring me something though."

Monica placed the bag on Stevens's desk.

Stevens slipped on a pair of reading glasses and pulled the bag toward her. "What's this? A napkin?"

Monica felt her face flush as she explained how she'd found the napkin at Kiran's Soul Spring Spa.

Stevens gave her an odd look but all she said was "Go on."

"I overheard Candi Clawson admitting to the murder of her

mother. I think that napkin is evidence. It's what she used to suffocate Jolie."

"I'll send it to forensics to see if they can lift any DNA from it." She licked some cream cheese off her finger. "Meanwhile, it wouldn't hurt to bring Candi Clawson in to answer a few questions."

"What about that bottle of Thermodynamics I brought in. Any news?"

"Not yet, I'm afraid. But I'll let you know when I hear something."

"There's something else." Monica cleared her throat. "Kiran, whose real name is Alex Timmerman, worked as a home health aide for Loving Hands Hospice. Several clients claimed that he had stolen from them and one woman, Philippa Thomas, thinks he scared her mother to death."

Stevens's face had clouded over. "Sounds like he's an all-around scoundrel." She placed her elbows on her desk and laced her fingers together. "Hopefully we can nail him on the drug charge. We have been working overtime trying to crack this drug ring that's sprung up lately. Unfortunately, I think it's too late to prove he was responsible for those thefts. As for scaring that woman to death, I don't know how we could possibly prove that."

Monica left Stevens's office feeling disappointed. She felt sick at the thought of Kiran getting away with what he'd done but she understood Steven's point. How could they prove anything so long after the fact? There was nothing to be done unless that bottle of Thermodynamics proved to contain cocaine. Then they'd at least be able to nail him on drug charges.

She looked at her watch. There was still time to pop into the library to return some books. She glanced in her rearview mirror and noticed that a gray Kia Forte was behind her. She and Greg had test driven one, but despite the persuasive arguments of the salesman, she'd decided to nurse her Ford Focus along as long as possible.

She pulled into the library parking lot and was surprised to see that the Kia was pulling in behind her. She parked, retrieved the books from the backseat and walked up the path to the front door.

An old house had been converted into the Cranberry Cove Library. Monica always enjoyed its sense of coziness and hominess. She couldn't linger today, although she did cast an eye over the shelf of new books as she walked to the desk.

Phyllis Bouma, the librarian, looked up from her computer, where she was entering information on new acquisitions. "How's that new baby doing? Sleeping through the night yet?"

"Just about. I can't believe how fast he's growing."

Phyllis nodded. "Next thing you know, you'll be waving goodbye as he goes off to college."

Monica deposited the books in the book return. She glanced at her watch. "I'd better hurry. Greg is with Teddy and is going to have to leave for an estate sale in a few minutes."

She waved goodbye to Phyllis and hurried to her car. She was about to put it in gear when the passenger-side door was wrenched open and Candi Clawson slid onto the front seat.

"Drive."

"Get out of my car."

Candi pulled a gun from her purse. "Drive."

"Where?" Monica's voice quivered.

"Toward that field where Timmy was killed. You know what I mean."

"You killed him, didn't you?" Monica said as she put on her blinker. "Because he was cheating on you."

"I'd given up so much for him. My mother never liked him. She ratted him out to the police and he went to jail. When he got out, we started seeing each other again. On the sly. But my mother found out and she cut off my allowance."

Monica slowed at the traffic light, but before she could stop the light turned green. Candi had nothing to lose by killing her. She had to find a way to get her out of the car or to even jump out herself. There weren't any more stops coming up any time soon. Could she stall the car? But then she'd still have to get away somehow and she knew she couldn't outrun a bullet.

Her hands were slippery on the wheel and one by one she wiped them on her pants. She had to get away for Teddy's sake. The thought made her feel faint. *Concentrate!*

They'd already passed the downtown area, the familiar storefronts whizzing by in a haze.

"You killed your mother, didn't you?" Monica said, risking a quick glance at Candi. The gun was resting in her lap with her finger still through the trigger guard.

"I didn't have any money." Candi's voice rose to a whine. "And my mother had inherited all that money from that old man she married. She could have given me some—she wouldn't have even missed it—but she told me I needed to get a job and support myself. I don't have any qualifications. What would I end up doing? Waiting tables? Dealing with drunks in a bar again? Cleaning up people's filth in their houses or motel rooms?

"She said that's what she did. She said being a home health aide was no picnic."

"Maybe if you had gotten a job, proved yourself, your mother would have changed her mind and shared the inheritance with you. But it's too late now."

"Yeah. I thought when she died I'd inherit the money, or at least part of it, but instead it went back to those Spencer girls. And when Timmy found out I wasn't getting the money after all, he took up with that other girl." She let out a sob. "He said he'd never loved me at all."

"So, killing Jolie didn't do you any good."

Candi let out a laugh that sent a shiver down Monica's spine. "No, but I had the satisfaction of watching her die. That was something at least."

Monica's hands tightened on the wheel. She had to keep herself together and she had to think. There had to be something she could do to save herself.

Then it came to her. They were even headed in the right direction. Her spirits lifted slightly. It might be her only chance. She couldn't blow it.

They were almost to the hill that led away from town. Monica's hands were trembling and she nearly swerved over the white line. It was now or never.

She prayed the patrol car that was almost always there was there today, patiently waiting to pounce on speeders. She was tempted to close her eyes as they approached the rise but then she spotted the black-and-white patrol car tucked off to the side of the road.

As soon as she saw it, she hit the gas and watched as the speedometer quickly climbed from a sedate thirty miles per hour to forty, fifty, sixty miles per hour.

"What are you doing?" Candi screamed, bracing herself with one hand against the glove compartment.

Monica prayed the road would continue to be empty of cars. The needle was hovering at seventy miles per hour when Monica heard a siren in back of her. She put her blinker on and stepped on the brake.

"What are you doing?" Candi screeched again. "Keep going."

"If I do, he's going to chase us and will probably radio ahead for backup. Just act naturally and for heaven's sake, hide that gun."

Monica pulled onto the shoulder of the road and eased the car to a stop. She rolled down her window in anticipation.

The officer approached, a book of tickets already in his hand. He stopped at the side of the car and pushed his hat back on his head. "License please."

Monica grabbed her handbag from the passenger well, pulled out her wallet and slipped out her driver's license. She passed it to the officer.

"I'm sorry, Officer. I shouldn't have been going so fast. My . . . my heel got stuck on the gas pedal and I couldn't get it free."

The patrolman looked unimpressed and continued writing on his pad. He handed Monica's license back to her and tore off the ticket.

Monica reached for it. "I promise it won't happen again." Then she gave the signal she'd seen on the evening news, folding her thumb across her palm and covering it with her fingers.

The officer nodded almost imperceptibly, his eyes serious as he scanned the interior of the car.

"What are you doing waving at him," Candi hissed as Monica put on her blinker and eased back onto the road.

Her heart was hammering so hard she was surprised Candi couldn't hear it. Had the patrolman gotten the message? He seemed to have but perhaps that was simply wishful thinking on her part.

She continued to drive at the sedate and law-abiding pace of thirty miles per hour. She stared into the distance but didn't see anything out of the ordinary. They'd soon be at the field where Timmy had been killed. She had no doubt what Candi's plan was for her.

The field was coming into view and Monica was beginning to despair. It looked as if the cavalry wasn't going to arrive after all. Maybe the patrolman had misunderstood her hand gesture or he didn't know the meaning of it. If that was the case, she was on her own.

"Pull over," Candi said, waving the gun for emphasis.

Loose rocks rumbled under the wheels of the Focus as Monica did what she was told. Candi kept the gun aimed at Monica's head as she ordered her from the car.

The wind had a chilly edge to it but despite that, Monica was sweating.

"Walk," Candi commanded. Monica felt the gun pressed into her side.

They weren't far from the road when Candi's foot caught on a tangle of weeds, sending her sprawling. The gun flew from her hand and landed several feet away.

Monica dove for it just as Candi began to crawl toward it. Monica's fingertips brushed the barrel of the gun but Candi was closer. Her hand closed around the handle and she pulled it out of Monica's grasp.

Candi stumbled to her feet and Monica did the same, brushing dirt and grass from her knees. Once again, Candi began to force her to walk across the field. She had no idea where they were going but she knew she didn't want to be out of sight of the road.

Candi was about to take a step forward when she gave a high-pitched scream and stumbled backward. She tripped and landed flat on her back.

Monica looked to see what had scared her and saw a snake coiled in the grass, one that Monica recognized as a garter snake by the yellow stripe down its side.

As Candi was trying to get to her feet, she momentarily put the gun down and Monica didn't waste a second. She pounced.

And now the tables were turned. Monica stood over Candi, the gun in her hand. She wasn't sure what she was going to do, when she heard sirens in the distance, getting louder as they got closer.

Three patrol cars pulled up alongside the field and uniformed men poured out of them. They began running toward Monica, their weapons drawn.

One of them had a bullhorn. "Put the gun down," he bellowed at Monica.

She carefully bent and placed it on the ground.

"It's the one on the ground," one of the patrolmen said.

Monica recognized him as the officer who had stopped her and given her a ticket. He had recognized the hand signal after all.

Two officers grabbed Candi by the arms and helped her to her feet. "Don't worry about that ticket," the one said and winked at her. "I'm not turning it in."

Monica heard a satisfying snap as they fastened handcuffs around Candi's wrists and began to march her over to the waiting patrol cars.

The scene suddenly went blurry and was fading to a haze. Monica felt her knees begin to buckle.

"Someone drive this young lady and her car home," one of the officers commanded. "Stevens can catch up with her there. Bruce"—he motioned to one of the other men—"follow them in your car."

Monica collapsed into the passenger seat of her Focus. Her hands hadn't stopped shaking since Candi had jumped into her car, and she was exhausted. She couldn't wait to get home to Greg and Teddy.

Chapter 24

Monica, Greg, Nancy, Jeff, Lauren, Gina and Estelle were gathered around the dining table in Monica and Greg's new house. The walls were bare, there were blank spots where furniture would eventually be placed and boxes were stacked against the wall waiting to be unpacked, but Monica thought it already felt like home.

Janice, Nora and Mick had all given them housewarming gifts and Tempest had sent a box of crystals—amethyst to bring relaxation to the bedroom, whimsical angel aura quartz for Teddy's room, citrine that Monica had placed on the kitchen windowsill to catch the sunlight and selenite for harmony in the living room.

Monica was serving up the chicken and rice casserole she'd made in her new kitchen when her cell phone rang. She went to silence it but then noticed the call was from Detective Stevens. She excused herself and went into the living room to take the call.

"Monica? I wanted to let you know we got the forensic report on the bottle of Thermodynamics powder you brought in. Only it's not any sort of supplement unless you count cocaine as a supplement."

So, she'd been right, Monica thought.

"The DNA test on the napkin hasn't come back yet but Candi Clawson admitted everything—killing her mother and boyfriend and trying to kill you. That was some pretty quick thinking on your part, by the way."

"Born of desperation. I couldn't think what else to do."

"It worked." She paused. "I won't keep you. I wanted to fill you in on the results of that test."

Monica rejoined her guests at the dinner table.

"Was that Detective Stevens?" Gina helped herself to a glass of wine.

"Yes. Bad news. The powder in that jar of Thermodynamics turned out to be cocaine, as we'd expected."

Gina's face fell. "I guess that means that the Soul Spring Spa will be closing."

"Maybe someone else will buy it." Monica poured herself some wine.

"Or they'll rent the space out to some dull and dreary business like a dry cleaner."

"The drug scheme was quite clever." Monica took a sip of her sauvignon blanc. "Lou at Johnny-on-the-Spot received the drugs and passed them along in the porta-potties to the two dealers, one of them being Kiran. Kiran cut the cocaine and placed it in bottles with the Thermodynamics label, making it look legitimate. He then sold the drugs to someone who would peddle them on the street."

"I saw on the news that they arrested someone for the murder of that poor woman who was stuffed in the porta-potty at Jeff and Lauren's wedding." Nancy reached for the salt.

"Yes." Monica spooned some of the chicken casserole onto her plate. "Her daughter killed her because she needed money and she thought she would inherit from Jolie when she died."

"What is that saying?" Greg said. "Something about money being the root of all evil."

Monica cocked an ear. There was a rustling sound on the baby monitor and she held her breath but all was quiet. Teddy was obviously sleeping soundly.

"This has got me thinking and I've had a brilliant idea." Estelle clapped her hands together. "Why don't I buy the Soul Spring Spa? I can hire someone to teach the classes." She linked her arm through Gina's. "Then I won't have to leave my lovely daughter-in-law. We'll have such fun."

"It will be an adventure," Gina agreed.

Monica, Greg, Nancy, Jeff and Lauren looked at each other. It was obvious they were all thinking the same thing.

Oh, no.

Recipe

Cranberry Banana Bread

1½ cups all-purpose flour plus 1 tablespoon
1 teaspoon baking soda
1 teaspoon salt
3 ripe bananas, mashed
1 cup white sugar
1 egg
¼ cup melted butter
1 cup fresh cranberries
½ cup chopped walnuts (optional)

Preheat oven to 325 degrees.

Grease a 9x5-inch loaf pan.

Mix 1½ cups flour, baking soda and salt in a bowl.

In another bowl, combine bananas, sugar, egg and melted butter.

Add dry mixture to wet mixture and stir well.

Toss cranberries with 1 tablespoon flour.

Gently fold cranberries and walnuts into batter.

Bake for approximately one hour.

About the Author

Peg grew up in a New Jersey suburb about twenty-five miles outside of New York City. After college, she moved to the City, where she managed an art gallery owned by the son of the artist Henri Matisse.

After her husband died, Peg remarried and her new husband took a job in Grand Rapids, Michigan, where they now live (on exile from New Jersey, as she likes to joke). Somehow Peg managed to segue from the art world to marketing and is now the manager of marketing communications for a company that provides services to seniors.

She is the author of the Cranberry Cove Mysteries, the Lucille Mysteries, the Farmer's Daughter Mysteries, the Gourmet De-Lite Mysteries, and also, writing as Meg London, the Sweet Nothings Vintage Lingerie series, and as Margaret Loudon, the Open Book series.

Peg has two daughters, a stepdaughter and stepson, and two beautiful granddaughters. You can read more at pegcochran.com and meglondon.com.

Made in the USA
Middletown, DE
18 August 2024